A Summer Morning

A Novel By

Anne Leigh Parrish

To John, Bob, Lauren, Lacey, and Sam

Contents

A Summer Morning

Chapter One

The solstice was tomorrow, and the twilight stretched on and on. Even if you stood and watched it closely, gauging the gradual loss of color from the sky, you never saw the final coming of night. The day just disappeared. Timothy had lived in upstate New York all his life and hated summer. As a child, he suffered terribly from sunburn and mosquito bites and would sweat so much that his skin never felt dry. There was more truth in cold than in heat, more honor in darkness than in light. He never told anyone he felt that way. He couldn't imagine how it would ever come up. It was his secret, one that set him apart. Grief did that, he thought. It made us who we are.

Timothy lifted his head and glanced out the living room window. Sure enough, the light was gone.

Sam washed the dishes. Something was on her mind. She was quiet during dinner, asking only if he liked her meatloaf. He always did, but this one was particularly good. She cooked well, though her repertoire was limited. Meatloaf showed up once a week. So did pork chops, and tuna noodle casserole.

Timothy went into the kitchen and asked if she needed help.

She turned off the faucet. Drops of water fell from her fingertips onto the braided rug at her feet.

"You know, I really do want a baby," she said.

She hadn't brought it up since Christmas Eve when they came home from dinner at his mother's. Before that, it was around Halloween. Given her habit of raising the issue near a holiday, she was early. Independence Day was two weeks off.

"I know. And you know how I feel about that," he said.

"I think we need to talk about it."

"There's nothing to talk about."

"We've been together for three years. We're not jumping into anything here."

He took a chair at the table where they ate only an hour before. She dried her hands and sat, too. He met her eye because she hated it when he didn't. He ran his hand through his hair. It was beginning to thin. He was only thirty-four. He saw himself in ten years, bald and soft in the middle.

"I know children aren't convenient," Sam said. "But that's not why you have them."

"Then why?"

"Because your heart is full of love."

"You know I love you."

"Yes. And I also know you would love a baby."

"You need more than love to be a good father."

"True. And you have those things. You just don't want to think so."

Timothy's sister, Angie, just had a pregnancy scare, and that's why Sam was thinking about children again. Like Timothy, Angie didn't want any. As to her boyfriend, Matt, Timothy didn't know. They didn't talk about it. Angie was thirty-five now; Sam was thirty-two. Timothy's mother said women had to listen to their biological clocks. In his mother's case, her clock was set early. She had her first baby when she was nineteen.

"It's not a good idea," he said.

"Why?"

"Because it's not."

"You're just scared," she said.

"I just think we should wait."

"For what?"

"Something better."

"You always say that."

"I like being just the two of us."

Sam's eyes welled, but she didn't cry. She stared at the floor. She installed the black-and-white tiles herself a few months ago, a home improvement project that took much longer than she expected. She stuck with it though, working into the night for most of the week.

She went into the bedroom and closed the door.

Timothy returned to the living room, sat on the couch, and picked up the book he was reading about the Incas. The chapter he just began was on the practice of sacrificing humans to ward off earthquakes and floods. Quite often, the victims were children. The irony of that wasn't lost on him.

He closed the book and put it on the coffee table. He stood and went down the narrow hall to their bedroom. The door was ajar. He hadn't heard it open. Sam wasn't a quiet person. She sighed and hummed and cleared her throat as she went around the house. She wasn't light on her feet, either. She was tall, almost as tall as he was. He stood just under six feet. She used to be heavy and put herself on a strict low-carb diet the year before, the results of which were amazing, but she was still a commanding presence, and here she opened the door in total silence.

"Babe?" he said. He leaned into the room. She sat on the bed with her back to him, facing the black window where the branch of an oak tree scraped the glass. Her shoulders rose and fell. She wore a T-shirt that was now too big. He thought of the pleasant evening they would have had if she hadn't dumped her baby demands on him. Was it really because Angie had been late?

He entered the room.

"Hey," he said. He sat down beside her on the bed.

They were reflected in the glass. They looked like ordinary people, he thought. Like any man and woman wanting to remember how much they loved each other.

"I'm sorry," she said.

"It's okay."

She shook her head. Her red hair was thick and wavy. He wanted to gather it in his hands. For months she had wanted to cut it, and every time she said so he begged her not to.

"No, it's not," she said.

"I know."

She turned and stared at him. The blue iris of her right eye was flecked with black. He looked at the flecks, waiting until he couldn't wait anymore.

"Do you think if you had a baby I'd wake up and be someone else? And do what? Go into business, like Angie? Or apply to graduate school, like Foster?" he asked.

Sam sighed. She said once Timothy was jealous of his younger brother because he knew what he wanted and was willing to go after it. Timothy was jealous, but that wasn't the reason. Foster was the youngest—the baby of the family—and as such had the fewest expectations laid on him. He also had no one to answer to. Foster was single.

Timothy didn't like where his thoughts were going.

"I'm sorry. I shouldn't have said that," he said.

"It's all right. Lavinia does a good job of throwing your siblings in your face."

Lavinia was his mother and told him the other day he was the only one of her five children who was stuck. His twin sisters had that distinction for years, but now were gaining traction in their respective careers. Marta was an actress and had one good role after another. Maggie's paintings were on display in three galleries in New York City, where they shared an apartment. He thought they were both pampered and spoiled because despite their success they were still supported by their mother. Foster wanting to become a veterinarian gave him a big leg up, and Angie had always been golden in the achievement department. She put in ten years as a social worker before quitting to help Matt run his bar, but what made Lavinia's remark so hard was knowing Timothy was her favorite, and his shortcomings caused her acute disappointment.

He offered to finish the dishes for Sam. She said she'd do them in a bit. He asked if she just wanted to go on sitting there for a while.

"No," she said.

He ran his hand up and down her back. It was soft and fleshy before. Now it was firm. She used a Pilates ball she kept in the garage. The house was small, and there wasn't anywhere else to keep it. The spare room had a sofa bed, a desk, a chair, and his computer. He kept his photography equipment in there, too. He hadn't taken any pictures in a while. He didn't think he was any good at it, though some people, especially his mother, who bought him the digital camera and tripod, as well as a subscription to Photoshop, said he had talent and should just apply himself. When he looked through the viewfinder at whatever he was trying to capture he was excited. Then, when he took the shot and reviewed the image, he was disappointed. Nothing in the camera's memory looked like it did in real life. When he explained that to Sam she said he should edit the picture, or work with the variance from reality.

The wind rose and the tree branch danced. Sam sighed and stood up. She said she better get at those dishes because it was getting late.

"Wait," he said.

"What?"

"I'm sorry. Really."

"It's okay."

She left the room and he sat, listening to the tree branch.

Later, when he went into the kitchen, he found everything done. Their two mugs stood by the coffee machine, which she filled with coffee and water. In the morning all she had to do was press the "on" button.

Sam sat at the dining room table, which doubled as her workspace. She was a college student. She scribbled something in her journal. Another poem, no doubt. She wrote brilliant poems, according to her record of getting them published. She used a pencil on blank paper. She didn't like lines because they were too confining. She lifted her head to look out the window. She couldn't see him from where she sat. She cried and wiped her eyes with her hand. Then she got back to work.

"Hey," he said.

"Oh, you startled me! What are you doing?"

"Just coming to see how you are."

"I'm fine. Just finishing this up."

"Well, this working man should head to bed." He glanced at the cabinet where he kept a bottle of bourbon. He could use a drink.

"Okay. I'll be in soon."

He blew her a kiss. She didn't see it because she went back to her page.

He got into bed and thought about Sam having a baby. He could see her as a mother. She had the right instincts. But a baby would keep them up all night. And the diapers! There were so many cons. Why couldn't she see that? They didn't need a baby. A baby was the last thing they needed.

His mind wandered.

He thought about Sue, his co-worker at the GAP store where he worked. She had a crush on him. He liked watching her try to hide it. He hated it, too. All that pain of wanting what she wasn't going to get.

"Why don't we go out sometime?" she asked just the other day.

"Because you're married."

She threw her dark hair over her shoulder, stood up straight, and sucked in her stomach. "And if I weren't?"

"My girlfriend wouldn't like it."

"The poet."

"I only have one."

"You look like you'd enjoy having two."

A customer came up to the counter with five pairs of blue jeans and she turned away.

Sue wasn't much. Just another lonely person. She lost a baby around Christmas. A few weeks before that, Timothy found her throwing up in the sink in the employee breakroom and she explained why she was sick. He didn't need to know. It bothered him that she told him. It assumed an intimacy they didn't have, one she wanted to create and tightened later when she told him she had a miscarriage.

But he liked flirting with her.

A lot of women found him attractive. And he could have been with anyone he wanted, and he wanted Sam.

Sam was no stunning beauty, but there was something about her that soothed his heart. She brought peace into the room when she entered it, and the peace stayed on for a while after she left.

Lavinia said he didn't want children because he didn't want to share Sam. She went on to add that a child expanded one's life, and when a woman became a mother she had more love in her to go around than she did before. Lavinia wanted to be a grandmother, and that's why she was making up all that nonsense. When Timothy was a kid, she was as mean as hell. She worked too hard, he understood that. His father had been useless, and the burden of earning money and raising children fell to her. Hindsight is twenty-twenty, he thought, because she was simply describing how she wished she felt, herself, back in the day. Sam and Lavinia hadn't gotten along for quite a while, then one of them softened toward the other and now they were great friends.

He stirred when Sam came to bed. The cucumber scent of her face soap was comforting. She pulled the quilt up over her shoulder. It was an antique she found the year before, sewn by hand, with rings of blue and gold. They only used it in the spring and summer. It was too light to keep them warm at night in winter.

Dawn came before he was ready to wake. They neglected to lower the blind, and the east-facing window screamed with sunshine. Sam was cheerful over coffee. She looked forward to the weekend. There was a picnic planned out at the lake.

"Yeah? Who's going?" Timothy asked.

"Matt, Angie, of course. Your mom. I think Foster's coming. Your dad. Maybe Alma, but I think she'd rather stay home."

Alma was Lavinia's live-in housekeeper and close friend. After Lavinia's second husband died, they had the house to themselves. It was a big old barn. Then Potter, Timothy's dad, moved in the year before when his second marriage went bust. None of the children understood how their long-divorced parents could live under the same roof, but they seemed to be making a go of it. Potter was Matt's partner, and co-owner of their bar, The Watering Hole. He also worked there.

"What are we bringing?" Timothy asked. The idea of being surrounded by familiar faces made his left temple throb.

"I don't know. What do you want me to make?"

"Up to you. Your chicken salad is always a winner."

"Good idea."

Sam smiled at him. Her eyes were bright and clear. She made peace with the sorrow of yesterday evening, but then he thought not. It was merely waiting quietly in a corner of her heart.

"Curry style, right?" he asked, meaning the chicken salad.

"Of course. Though I don't think Matt cares for it."

"He'll be okay."

She nodded, looked at the paper, and said a poet from New York City was coming up to give a reading. He saw her wondering if she should attend. She went to several readings and found them hard. She loved hearing new imagery and wordplay yet sank into doubting her own abilities and aesthetic afterward.

"I could tag along if you want," he said.

"To what? The reading? I thought you said you'd never go."

"I'll keep an open mind."

He realized his mistake. But if she thought of making a segue back to the baby thing, she said nothing. Nor did she give herself away. That woman had a hell of a good poker face sometimes.

"It's a week from Friday," she said.

"Great."

He stood up and put his coffee cup in the sink. Then he bent and kissed her on the cheek.

"Have a good day," he said.

"You, too."

His car was slow to start. It was a 1965 Mercedes Benz two-seater he bought for a song and had been pouring money into ever since. He loved driving it. The manual transmission and the soft, worn leather seats always improved his mood. The steering wheel was white and reminded him of a pearl. Sam said it left a huge carbon footprint. She drove a tiny Toyota Scion that sipped gas when she drove at all. She biked a lot, even to the store, with a backpack to carry groceries.

Fridays were good days. It had taken a long time for the former store manager to give him weekends off. Now he was the manager, a position he didn't like but could easily handle. Back in college, he saw himself doing something exalted, in the arts or even politics. His stepfather, Chip, encouraged the latter. The three sons from his first marriage hadn't been interested. Chip had ambitions of his own. He spoke yearningly of becoming mayor. Lavinia said she'd do her part and organize the campaign. That put an end to the idea. Lavinia was competent and practical, just the wrong person to get involved in something you'd rather go on dreaming about. Chip lost interest in Timothy's vague plans when he got arrested for shoplifting a leather jacket. He could afford it and took it just for fun. At Lavinia's insistence, Chip got his record expunged, which made the job he found at the GAP possible. Sam said Timothy's love of risky behavior wasn't healthy and spoke to a deep self-hatred. He didn't argue with her.

The neighborhood was a wall of green. The lawns were tidy, except for a few where the grass was tall and wild. Sam mowed their yard. She enjoyed doing it. A man stood in his driveway and waved when Timothy passed by. Timothy didn't know him, but he waved back. As he came around the corner a bicyclist rode in the center of the lane. Timothy honked. The rider veered onto the shoulder and shouted something angry. Timothy flipped her off. Then he thought of Sam and the bad drivers she complained about. A car almost hit her the year before. She could have been killed.

Timothy turned right at the next corner and circled back. The bicyclist was still riding on the shoulder, heading in the same direction she was when Timothy went by before. He slowed, reached over to roll down the passenger side window of the car, and came alongside her.

"I'm sorry about that," he called out. The bicyclist swung her head to the left and stared at him. She stopped riding. He pulled onto the shoulder in front of her. He turned off the engine and sat a moment, watching her in the rearview mirror. He got out and stood by the car.

"I'm sorry," he called out again.

"You're a maniac," the woman said. She had an accent. Something Scandinavian. He approached her and she pulled out her cell phone.

"I'm going to call the police if you don't leave me alone," she yelled.

Timothy held up his hand.

"Look, I'm just trying to say I'm sorry for honking at you back there."

She stood, breathing hard. She was petite and well-muscled. Her expression was fierce. She removed her helmet, revealing a perfectly round head that had recently been shaved. He thought wearing the helmet must be uncomfortable. He approached. She dismounted and lay the bicycle on the ground after removing the water bottle from its holster and taking a long drink.

She stared at him. "I know you," she said. Her accent was Russian, not Scandinavian.

"I don't think so."

"You're Teemothy Dugan. We were in class together at university."

He thought back. He couldn't place her.

"Geology 101," she said, and he recalled a huge lecture hall stuffed with students. The exams had been multiple-choice. He never studied yet pulled off a B-.

"How did we know each other?" he asked.

"We didn't. But I knew you. Everybody did."

It was true he had a reputation then. He lived in a fraternity and partied every night. He organized elaborate pranks on rival houses that involved enlisting all the brothers who could carry a tune, lining them up below bedroom windows, and giving forth with true stage presence. A compact disc player was often used to provide the necessary instrumental background. He wasn't resented for it. He was too good-humored for that. The pleasant demeanor was all an act. He was miserable in college, often depressed, and fearful of the future. And here the future was, just as unfulfilling as he suspected it would be. Sam floated through his mind, and he felt even worse. Whenever he talked like that, about his forebodings, her jaw squared and her gaze narrowed.

"What's your name?" Timothy asked.

"Svetlana."

"Well, Svetlana, I'm sorry I honked at you. It was awfully rude."

"Is okay. You call me sometime. We go out."

"I don't think so."

"Married?"

"Yes."

"No ring."

"I lost it."

"Wife must be mad."

"You should have heard her!"

He returned to his car. Svetlana picked up her bike, mounted it, put her helmet on, and cycled off. She waved as she went by.

Timothy held the steering wheel. Why did he lie about being married? For the same reason he always lied. It sounded good. Only it didn't.

"Being a decent guy isn't always easy. There are temptations, choices, and unseen consequences," his dad, Potter, once said. They were in a bar. Potter was getting smashed. Timothy was helping him. Potter's wife, Mary Beth, had been calling him on his cell for the previous hour. Finally, Potter turned off the phone.

"But really, it all comes down to the same thing. Don't be a jerk," Potter said and knocked back his shot of bourbon.

Because of Svetlana, Timothy was late. Jimmy, the part-time college kid was in the back, staring at a stack of boxes that were just delivered.

"Where's Sue?" Timothy asked.

"Beats me."

Timothy went into his tiny office, picked up the phone, and listened to voice mail. Sue left a message just after six that morning saying she had the flu and couldn't come in. She sounded awful, hoarse, and congested, so he figured she was telling the truth. Timothy returned to Jimmy and asked him if he had coffee yet. Jimmy said he hadn't. He looked hungover.

Timothy took a ten out of his wallet and told him to go hit up the Starbucks in the mall. Jimmy stared at the bill in his hand.

"I'll open the boxes and see what we got, then when you come back, you can help me unpack them," Timothy said.

Jimmy wandered off.

Timothy thought for months about firing him and couldn't bring himself to. He reminded him so much of himself at that age. Just a good-hearted guy who liked to have a little too much fun.

Timothy took the box cutter from the drawer and went into the storeroom. He slit the packing tape on one box and looked inside. Baby clothes. He ordered these months before, but something or other was out-of-stock and he got an apologetic phone call from someone in Central Shipping who said they'd be along soon.

He went back onto the floor to the children's section. On a shelf were small featureless mannequins who'd been wearing last year's rompers since spring. When Jiao came in, he'd ask her to pick out some new outfits and get them installed. Then he remembered she said she'd be a little late today because she was getting her nose pierced. Employees weren't supposed to wear nose rings or studs, but Timothy allowed it. No one from Corporate had been in all year, and if someone did make an unannounced visit, he'd remind them Dunston was a college town, and facial piercings were as common as toast. Timothy was pretty sure Jiao was a lesbian, at least she showed no interest in him. He knew it was shallow of him to think like that, but he was used to trusting his instincts.

Sam wanted to put a diamond stud in one nostril. When she asked him what he thought, he made a face. Her expression darkened, and he said he thought it was fine. She didn't do anything about it, but one of these days he'd come home, and there it would be. When Sam raised something and he didn't agree, she went ahead anyway. That's what she did when she wanted to change the bathroom wall color. She suggested a soft rose shade, and he said he preferred plain white. She painted it herself one day when he was at work. When she showed it to him, he thought it looked awful, but said she did a great job and thanked her for tackling it.

"Jesus Christ," he said to the empty store.

Was Sam pregnant? Another *fait accompli* he'd have to live with? No. She raised it before and nothing happened. No shy little smile followed by, "Guess, what?" Was she still taking her pills? He didn't know. He never saw her do it. No, wait, she got an IUD the year before because it was easier than remembering to do something every day. Did she go to the doctor and have it removed?

He told himself to calm down, but the idea had taken hold of him now, and he felt like hell. Sam might decide to get pregnant and follow through—with or without him.

Chapter Two

The next morning, Timothy woke early. Remembering it was the solstice, he thought everything was going to be all right. The days would start to shorten, and tonight, after the picnic, he and Matt were going up to Syracuse to hear a band Matt might want to book for The Hole. He felt bad when he realized he hadn't told Sam.

He mentioned it over coffee. She lifted her eyes and stared at him for a long moment. She was unhappy about the short notice, he could tell.

"Sounds like fun," she said.

"Why don't you come, too?"

"What time are you guys heading up there?"

"I don't know. I'll ask Matt when we get to the lake."

"Cool."

Was she serious? Would she go? She was working on a crossword puzzle at the moment, and he couldn't read her expression.

Sam was quiet on the drive out to the lake. They took her car, and as always, he was uncomfortable. His legs cramped in the short footwell space. He fidgeted this way and that, and she suggested he push his seat back. He lifted the lever with his right hand and the seat slid silently, giving him much more space to stretch out.

"I don't know why that never occurred to me," he said.

"I mention it every time."

That was true. She did.

He reached out and rested his hand on her shoulder.

"What's that for?" she asked, as she slowed for a stop sign.

"My eternal affection for you."

She laughed. "I'm the one who's supposed to be flowery."

Her poetry wasn't exactly that. It was elegant, to be sure. Full of grace and wisdom. But not flowery. She referred to something else, some personal trait, or how she dressed, though she tended to confine herself to T-shirts and blue jeans. Today she wore a peasant blouse she picked up at the farmers' market. It was hand-sewn with red and blue thread. The cuffs on the long sleeves had pearl buttons. The jeans were replaced with a denim skirt that fell to her ankles. Sam didn't like her legs, even now, after the weight loss. Timothy didn't understand why. She had great legs.

The road followed the long curve of the shoreline. The water was blue and calm, perfect sailboat weather, though he didn't know how to sail. He should learn. He could take lessons. And when he mastered it, he could buy a boat. He had money. Chip remembered all the kids in his will, though probably not to an equal extent. Lavinia knew exactly who got how much and refused to say. The siblings never discussed it among themselves, either. Timothy suspected he got less than the others, though he had no good reason to think so.

But blowing his inheritance on a boat would be stupid.

The parking lot was filling up fast. They saw Lavinia's car, a mud-splattered Land Rover, in a space next to the beach path, and pulled in behind it to unload. Lavinia always got to these things first to stake out a table. As Timothy was bringing out the bowl of chicken salad, she walked briskly toward them up the path. She had on a huge straw hat and designer sunglasses that made her look like a movie star. Her toenails were painted sky blue. They matched the shawl which hung casually around her shoulders.

"Good. Now you can keep me company," she said and took the bowl out of Timothy's hands.

"No Alma?"

"She's getting her hair done."

Sam waited until they were clear, then backed up and headed off to find a place to park. Timothy followed Lavinia to the table she chose, which was close to the water in the shade of a huge oak tree, near a barbeque grill. On it was a plastic tablecloth patterned with strawberries. It was from Timothy's childhood. He hadn't seen it in years, and the meals around it, usually with Potter in his cups, returned. Where was Potter, anyway?

Timothy asked.

"Who knows? He was supposed to be here half an hour ago. He said he had to swing by the store first. Didn't even call to say he was running late," Lavinia said.

"Do you have your notifications on? I know you sometimes turn them off."

Lavinia took her phone out of the pocket of her jeans and stared at it. "He texted, 'the place is packed, line's long, on my way soon.'"

She took a seat at the end of the bench facing the water. She asked if the bowl Timothy brought contained chicken salad. He said it did.

"Good cook, Sam," Lavinia said.

"She is."

"Good poet."

"That, too."

"She's made your home very pleasant."

"What is this, 'Praise Sam Day?'"

"Don't be flippant. You know everything I said is true."

"I'm not arguing."

Timothy wished he had a drink.

Sam arrived. She carried a tray of cut-up vegetables. "You forgot this," she said. She put the tray on the table. Lavinia stared at it. "Angie's bringing the dip," Sam added.

"What's his name?" Lavinia asked.

Sam chuckled and sat down.

"You like him, don't you?" Sam asked Lavinia.

"Who, Matt? Yes. I think he's just peachy."

"He's cute as hell, no denying," Sam said.

Since when did Sam think Matt was cute? She never said so. Timothy never heard her compliment another man's looks. He didn't think she even really liked Matt. Maybe she didn't like him, just his looks.

"Is anyone bringing beer?" Timothy asked.

"The cooler's over there," Lavinia said, indicating a patch of ground at the far end of the table. Timothy went over and lifted the lid. Sitting in a bed of ice were a bottle of white wine, several bottles of beer, and inexplicably, a bottle of champagne. He lifted the champagne and got Lavinia's attention.

"I thought someone might want to celebrate something," she said.

"Are they getting married?" Sam asked.

"Who?" Timothy asked.

"Matt and Angie, who else?" Sam asked.

She was quiet for a moment. She looked at Lavinia. "Not you and Potter," she said. Lavinia's impassive expression gave way to a small, sly smile.

"Jesus," Timothy said. "Are you *serious?*"

"You know he's the only man I ever loved," Lavinia said.

"Oh, my god."

"I think that's beautiful," Sam said.

Lavinia hastened to say that she had cared a great deal for Chip, more than she knew. She had trouble expressing her affection. She had to confront that she may have made him unhappy a lot of the time. She hoped wherever he was now, he forgave her.

Timothy wasn't used to his mother taking a metaphysical turn in her conversation.

"So, Potter is the love of your life," Sam said.

Lavinia nodded.

"Well, here's the love of mine," Sam said and extended her hand toward Timothy, who was still at the end of the table, holding the champagne. He put it down and picked up a beer.

Sam looked at the bottle, then at Timothy.

"Would you like one, too?" he asked her.

"Sure. Thanks."

He got her the beer. The top required an opener, which was sitting in a basket on the table along with plastic forks and knives. Next to the basket was a stack of paper plates and a package of napkins. Sam took the opener, used it on her beer, then handed it to Timothy who stared at it a moment before taking it. He sat down.

"Mom. Are you sure?" he asked.

"The short answer is yes. The long answer is I'm not getting any younger and neither is he."

"But what about, you know . . . ?"

"Sex?"

"Christ! I was talking about his drinking."

Sam laughed. She told Timothy he had a dirty mind.

"I can handle his drinking. *If* he falls off the wagon, that is. He's been holding steady for a while now," Lavinia said.

When she realized Sam and Timothy were staring at her, she asked them who could better deal with his lapses. She wasn't such a fool as to think they'd never happen again, even though he came home from The Watering Hole every night sober. Maybe he had a nip here and there. It didn't matter. She didn't care.

"Mom. You're in denial," Timothy said.

"No, dear, I'm in love."

Sam made a soft, cooing sound Timothy took for a swoon of affection. He drank his beer.

Angie's voice drifted over from the parking lot. "No, I never said that," she said.

Matt mumbled something in reply. Timothy tensed. His sister knew how to ruin a day.

She appeared wearing a black T-shirt and blue satin pants. She always dressed badly. Her hair had grown out since the last time Timothy saw her. Her bangs, a bizarre addition last winter, were tucked sloppily behind her ears. She carried a small cooler she set roughly on the table. Matt had on a button-down shirt and blue jeans. Timothy watched Sam to see if she were checking him out, but she was already drawn into a conversation with Angie, who took the seat next to her. Matt put down a couple of packages of hamburger buns. He said hello to Lavinia, Sam, and Timothy then sat down next to Lavinia, who told him was looking as dashing as ever.

"You look pretty spiffy, yourself," Matt said. Lavinia gave him her best smile. She asked how things were going down at the bar. Matt said it was a little slow since the university let out, but the summer school students were due next week, and then things would pick up. Potter was a great help. He took over ordering, a chore Matt didn't care for at all.

"Oh? I thought Angie was doing that," Lavinia said.

At the mention of her name, Angie turned to her mother and said, "We thought it would be better if Dad handled it." The way she said it meant they were trying to keep him usefully occupied. Angie said before Potter knew all the townies who came in regularly, and sometimes he liked to join them in a beer. Clearly, this was a way to keep him back in the office, out of harm's way.

"And what about you? Are you still enjoying it there?" Lavinia asked Angie.

"Yup."

"You don't miss Lindell?"

"Sometimes."

Lindell was the retirement home where Angie used to work as a social worker. Sam worked there, too, cleaning rooms, but only for a few months before she started school.

"I never could see being around old people," Timothy said.

"They're like anybody else. Besides, we're all heading that way," Angie said.

Lavinia asked when Foster was due to show. Her answer was met with confused silence.

"Didn't one of you call him and let him know about the picnic?" she asked the group.

"You said you'd do it," Angie said to Matt.

"No, I didn't."

"Yes, you did."

"Oh, honestly," Lavinia said and pulled out her phone. Just as she punched in Foster's number, he appeared alongside Potter carrying briquets and lighter fluid for the grill.

"Look who I found wandering around the store," Potter said and bent to kiss Lavinia on the cheek.

"Nice of you guys to let me know I was invited," Foster said.

"He was supposed to call you," Angie said, indicating Matt.

"I forgot. I'm sorry," Matt said.

"No problem," Foster said and sat down.

Potter and Matt went to set up the barbecue. Angie and Sam continued their conversation in low voices. Timothy wondered what was up. Foster helped himself to the six-pack of root beer Potter picked up at the store. He was the only one in the family who didn't drink. As far as Timothy knew, he never tasted alcohol. Foster was odd. He kept his thoughts to himself, which in their family was rare. He gave off an air of melancholy and had, even as a child. He was starting veterinary school in the fall, something he wanted to do for a long time. He adored animals. He was housesitting for a professor and his wife, and when they came back from Europe he moved into a new house where the landlord didn't allow pets. His cat, Mad Max, was living with Lavinia. She had some choice words to share about that in the beginning, but she was calmer about it now. Why didn't Lavinia buy Foster his own place? She could afford it, god knows. He probably could, too, with whatever sum he inherited. Maybe he didn't want to stay in Dunston. Sometimes he talked about leaving, but the vet he worked for—who encouraged him to apply to school—was helping with the tuition and promised him a job when he got his degree. Foster wouldn't let him down. He'd stick around until his informal debt was paid, however long that took.

The afternoon went on. Sam's chicken salad was eaten with delight. Matt overcooked the hamburgers and said his guy at The Hole would have done a much better job. Angie agreed, but she was nice about it.

Timothy was on his third beer when he noticed Sam giving him the evil eye. He drank it anyway, but more slowly. Finally, when everyone's energy had shifted to a lower gear, Potter stood up and announced that he and Lavinia had decided to give it another go. Matt congratulated them heartily; Angie sneered (or so it looked to Timothy); Sam was warm and optimistic; Foster looked stricken, but Timothy wasn't sure that was the cause. The champagne was opened. Timothy and Lavinia each had some in a paper cup. No one else wanted any.

Afterward, Potter suggested they all take a walk over to the waterfall on the other side of the park. Everyone wanted to go except Angie and Timothy.

"You sure?" Sam asked him.

"Yeah. I'll stay and help clean up."

Sam kissed him on top of the head and went off with the others. Timothy opened another beer.

"Why are you drinking so much?" Angie asked him.

"I'm not."

"Number four, plus champagne."

"You're keeping track?"

"I'm concerned."

"You don't need to be, I'm fine."

Angie looked skeptical. Timothy hoped she'd let it go. Once she got ahold of something, she held on tight. She ran them all ragged when they were children. As the eldest, she stood in for their mother. Her tongue was just as sharp. She gradually mellowed. Last winter, when she was making up her mind about Matt, she was withdrawn and anxious. Once she decided he wasn't the ogre she suspected he might be, she was overjoyed for a while, energetic, and fun to be around. Then she reverted to her default setting, a mood best described as grumpy. Matt, bless him, put up with it cheerfully. Sometimes Timothy didn't know how he stood it.

She got a beer for herself. She hadn't had any since she arrived. She asked how things were at work. He said they were the same. She said he hadn't been down to the bar much, lately. He said he liked it better during football season, or when a band was playing.

"Oh, speaking of bands, you're going with Matt tonight, right?" she asked.

"Yeah. Are you going?"

"Well, I was, but Sam invited me over, and I thought it would be cool to hang with just her for a while. You know, girls' night."

"When did she invite you?"

"I don't know. A couple of days ago."

"I only told her about the band this morning."

"I told her about it."

"Oh."

He could feel Angie wanting to say something and not finding a way. He asked her how she felt about their parents remarrying. She said she expected it. They were always devoted to each other, even in the bad times, she supposed. Their father was a good person—they all knew that, deep down. He just had a hard time with booze. Being afflicted with an addictive personality wasn't a crime. Lavinia understood that and would help him.

"How? With a stick?" Timothy asked.

"Come on."

"I was kidding."

Then Angie looked bemused. She was picturing it, he could tell.

"So, being at the bar's good?" Timothy asked.

"Mom already asked me that."

"Fine, now I'm asking."

She said it was okay. She didn't mind being on her feet all day, and she didn't mind waiting on people, either. Sometimes customers were jerks—never a regular, or someone they knew, but out-of-towners who complained about the food or that she was too slow getting their orders out. She told more than one if they didn't like it, not to come back.

"Wow. How does Matt feel about that?" Timothy asked.

"I have no idea."

Timothy laughed, despite himself.

"You must have a ton of jerks in your line of work," Angie said.

"All the time. But I'm not the owner's significant other, so I have to be polite."

"I'm always polite."

Timothy asked if it were hard being together at work, and then coming home together, too. Angie said that was one reason she was letting Matt go off to Syracuse.

"Letting?" Timothy asked.

"You know what I mean."

"Not preventing him."

"Right."

Angie held up her hand to indicate she didn't want to go where the conversation was headed. Timothy didn't want to, either, because he wanted to just sit and enjoy his beer buzz. When she stood up and began gathering the dirty plates to throw away, he helped her. They packed up the leftover food and folded up the tablecloth. Then there was nothing to do but wait for the others to come back. They went to the water's edge and watched children run in and out of the lake. One girl didn't want to go in, and some boys teased her about it. Angie told them to stop. A boy gave her the finger and Angie marched over to him and told him he was rude and one day it would get him a whole lot of trouble. Her tone was measured and easy as if she were talking about the weather.

"You can't bully people. How would you like it if someone did that to you?" Angie asked. The boy was overweight with short black hair. He stood with his arms crossed, obviously uncomfortable. Then Angie turned to the girl who was reluctant to go into the water and told her she didn't have to do anything she didn't want to do.

"Remember that—your whole life. When a boy wants you to do something that doesn't feel right, you don't have to," Angie said. Timothy stood, his empty beer bottle in his hand, watching her crusade.

Angie left the children and walked back to Timothy.

"Was that necessary?" he asked her.

"Yes."

The others returned. Lavinia and Potter were holding hands. Timothy felt queasy and wished he had more to eat. He hoped the place they were going to hear the band served food.

He carried the left-over bowl of chicken salad to Sam's car while she carried the tray that still had a lot of carrot sticks and celery. Then they returned to the table.

"We should just head up now," Matt told him.

"Yeah?"

"Show starts at six."

"It's only an hour's drive," Sam said.

"I want to get a good table. The place could get crowded."

"Okay. Well, if you get in super late, don't wake me up," Sam told Timothy.

Matt told Angie he'd see her later, and to have fun tonight.

"You, too," Angie said. "And behave yourself."

"Don't I always?"

"No." Then she kissed him on the mouth.

Timothy used the bathroom before they left. He looked at himself in the freckled mirror over the sink, where a rust stain rimmed the drain. His mother's dark coloring looked better on him than on her, though she was an attractive woman. So were Angie and his twin sisters. Foster, too, though they were all fair, like Potter. When he was growing up, his mother used to joke that she had Native American blood. His black hair and high cheekbones lent some truth to her remark.

Matt was waiting for him at the edge of the parking lot. They walked to his car, a used BMW, Timothy hadn't seen before.

"New ride," he said, and got in.

"Old one died."

"Miles?"

"Hundred and seventy-five thousand, but these things go forever."

"True."

The afternoon light was harsh. Matt remarked on it, and then said warm weather was on the way. He had to get the air conditioning unit repaired down at the bar or the customers would be all over him like white on rice. Timothy said summer would go by fast enough. At work, they were already talking about back-to-school sales.

"My mom never got a jump on that. Every year when I was a kid, I'd be the only one wearing a light jacket after the first snowfall," Matt said. He didn't grow up with a lot of money. His mother taught seventh-grade language arts, or something like that, Timothy couldn't remember. They compared their lousy childhoods more than once, and Timothy always got the unspoken prize for having a worse one. Thinking that brought him back to his parents getting together again. He asked Matt what he thought about it.

"True love can't be denied," he said.

"Spoken like a wise man."

"That's me."

Timothy asked about the band they were going to see and Matt said he didn't know much, just that they were a metal group. Timothy said it wasn't his favorite—he preferred something easier on the ear, like rhythm and blues, or even jazz, but he'd give it a try. He couldn't promise to stick it out if they sucked, and Matt agreed.

"We'll give them a couple of songs, then split," he said.

The open fields they drove past made Timothy uneasy. He wished the beer had calmed him more. He asked how things were going with Angie since she found out she wasn't pregnant.

"Oh, fine. She was relieved, but then they told her they think she's going through some sort of early menopause," Matt said.

"Wow. Really?"

"It happens, I guess. That's why she missed her period."

"Ah."

"Anyhow, just another little weirdness to stumble through."

"For sure."

Timothy asked Matt if he liked having her down at the bar every day. Matt said she was a huge help and had lots of good ideas about how to spruce the place up and improve the menu. She was a natural. And she understood people. She was great with the customers. Must be all those years in social work. A bar was this little community in itself, a microcosm of society, if you will, which he never really thought about before.

"Yeah," said Timothy. He wondered if Matt knew how she talked to some of the patrons.

"Your aunt owns a bar, doesn't she?" Matt asked.

"Patty? Yeah. In Montana."

"How did she end up there?"

"Didn't like it here, I guess. She left when she was about eighteen."

Patty was Potter's younger sister, and never said a good word about the dairy farm they grew up on. Timothy reflected that she was the only one in the family to go away for good. Somehow the twins didn't count, because they were still in the same state, though god knows, the bustle of Manhattan was different from the quiet academic atmosphere of Dunston.

He should get out of town and start somewhere new. Fresh vistas, and all that. He could finish that novel he tried to write, all about some miserable struggling artist—an alter-ego—not that he ever struggled as an artist, except for those few weeks banging away at a typewriter he bought at a thrift shop. His frat brothers thought he was nuts for not just getting a laptop, but they indulged him. He missed that comradery, that blanket acceptance. In some ways, he looked for it ever since.

"Do you ever feel like you just don't measure up?" Timothy asked.

"Whoa, that's a heavy question."

"Sorry."

"No worries. Um. Well, I screwed up a lot in my life, this we know. But not lately. I reckon I'm doing okay, generally speaking."

Timothy said he felt like he was disappointing people all the time.

"Yeah? Who?" Matt asked.

"I don't know. Everyone."

"Come on, man. You gotta be more specific than that. Are you talking about Sam?"

"Maybe."

"Why, what's going on?"

Timothy told him about her wanting a baby.

Matt said it was a natural thing to want. Then he guessed from the way Timothy was talking he didn't want one.

"I thought I didn't. But now I don't know. I mean, people do it all the time, right?" Timothy asked.

"Every day. Goes with the territory."

"What if you mess it up?"

"What, the kid?"

"Yeah."

"Kids are tough. I was. I'm sure you were, too. And from what I know of Sam's childhood, she's got us both beat, there."

Matt was right, Timothy thought. Sam came through in one piece.

"Kids are a scary idea, no doubt about it. Either you can take the plunge or you can't. Unless, of course, you knock someone up, she won't get rid of it, and you're too much in love to walk away," Matt said.

"Or too responsible."

"That, too."

"My mom thinks I'm being an idiot about it."

"Well, hell, she had five kids. Stands to reason."

They fell silent and didn't talk until they were pulling into Syracuse. Matt asked Timothy to get the address up on his phone and tell him where to go. The route took them through a seedy neighborhood, then a better one, and ended in a strip mall. The bar was next to a fast-food Mexican place. Timothy thought vaguely of getting himself a burrito, but Matt seemed to be in a hurry to get inside and scope the place out.

It took a moment for Timothy's eyes to adjust to the dark interior, and when they had, he saw it was a dump. The tables and chairs were old and scratched. The laminate floor was worn away in places. The bar itself was the one nice thing in the place—a solid piece with a huge mirror behind it, encased in carved wood. The glass shelves holding the liquor bottles were lit from below, making a cozy effect. In the back was a raised platform for the performers, just like the one at The Hole. A couple of guys were setting up sound equipment. They wore matching long-sleeved denim shirts and bolo ties. One guy had on a cowboy hat.

"Doesn't look like a metal band to me," Timothy said.

"Sure doesn't. Hang on." Matt went and talked to them. He came back.

"Country. Figures. Oh, well. You don't dig metal anyway, so it's all good, right?"

"Right."

Matt looked around the place. "Where is everybody?" he asked.

There were two customers at one table, and a guy by himself at the bar. But then a few more people came in, and then some more, and Timothy realized they were timing themselves around when the band was supposed to start. Matt grabbed a table set back a bit from the stage.

A server appeared.

"Holy crap," Matt said. Timothy looked up. The woman was a short brunette wearing a low-cut shirt and blue jeans.

"You got that right," the server said.

"What are you doing here?"

"What's it look like I'm doing here?"

"Oh, I'm sorry. Sharon, this is my good friend, Timothy. Timothy, Sharon."

"Hiya," Timothy said.

Sharon looked at them in a sly, hungry way.

"How did it work out, with the trial?" Matt asked.

"Case dismissed for lack of evidence."

"Wow. That's great."

"Yup."

"You like living up here?"

"It's great."

"Cool."

Sharon asked what they wanted to drink. Matt said he'd take a scotch and soda. Timothy asked for a margarita, no salt. Sharon nodded and left.

Matt explained Sharon used to work at The Hole last year and was arrested on suspicion of selling cocaine at the bar. She got out of it, obviously. She must have hired a good lawyer. The last time Matt heard, she had a public defender lined up, and those guys weren't always the best, so somebody, maybe their former boss, must have paid to get someone better, who specialized in drug cases, you know.

"Right," Timothy said.

Sharon brought their drinks. Matt asked if she knew when the band was going to play.

"No clue," she said.

When she left Timothy sipped his drink. It was watered-down, he could tell. Cheap bars served lousy drinks. That was a rule he never saw broken.

"You guys used to be tight?" he asked Matt.

"Not really."

"Didn't look that way to me."

"We were friends, that's all."

"She's cute, and I can see how you could have been more than that, but I'm not going to pry."

"I appreciate that."

He was lying, Timothy thought. He and that girl were more than friends. Angie said Matt used to have a drug problem. Sharon got arrested for selling cocaine. Maybe they partied together, too. It didn't matter as long as he cleaned himself up, which he seemed to have.

Matt drank his drink quickly. So did Timothy. He didn't care how drunk he got, as long as Matt could drive them home. He mentioned it.

"Hollow leg, remember?" Matt said.

"Just take it easy."

"Sure."

When Sharon came back to the table, Timothy ordered another drink. Matt didn't.

"That's not like you," Sharon told him.

"Things change."

"Things, not people."

"Bring the man his drink."

Sharon left. Matt looked angry for a moment, or he was just bored, waiting for the band. One of the musicians talked into the microphone and welcomed everyone. Some people clapped, but most didn't.

The music started and Timothy was borne away by the friendly, easy lilt of the vocalist. Sam liked country music. She lived in LA for a while and got a taste for it out there. He thought about her pretending not to know he made plans to come here with Matt. It didn't make sense.

After a couple of songs and another margarita, Timothy asked Matt if he'd try to book them at The Hole.

"I don't know," he said.

"You don't like them?"

"They're all right, I guess."

"They're great!

"I'm not sure our people would go for them."

"If you say so."

Timothy loved how the band alternated one upbeat song with a more melancholy, soulful one. Of course, the lyrics were all about love. One song was about a woman having a baby. The twinge he felt would have been a lot worse if he were sober.

Finally, Matt said he was ready to leave. He put down a couple of twenties on the table and pinned them under a salt shaker.

Timothy had to use the men's room. He liked what he saw in the mirror. If he were ever single again, he wouldn't be lonely long.

By the register, Matt and Sharon were talking. They stood close together, even though the band was taking a break and the noise level had dropped. Sharon's face lit up with a smile at something Matt said. He put his hand on her shoulder, and she swayed toward him. Then he kissed her, right on the mouth. It was a fast kiss, but unmistakable. Timothy wondered afterward if he saw what he thought he saw and knew he had, despite how much he had to drink.

Chapter Three

Sometimes summer was merciful, and when Timothy opened his eyes to an overcast sky, he was grateful. His head throbbed. Sam was in the kitchen, humming and making noise with pots and pans. He must have fallen back asleep because when he opened his eyes again, the light in the room had shifted and there was the smell of Sam cooking something.

He got up and pulled on a T-shirt and yesterday's boxers. His left instep hurt, and he wondered what he did to it.

Sam turned as he entered the kitchen.

"I thought you were going to sleep in," she said.

"What time is it?"

"A little after nine."

"Really? I thought it was the afternoon."

"Go back to bed."

"Nah. Just get me some coffee, would you?"

He sat down at the table and pawed vaguely at the newspapers. They subscribed to both the *Dunston Journal* and the *New York Times.* Sam loved reading the latter's book review. She hungrily absorbed what was being said about the latest poetry release. She had ambitions.

She asked how the band was.

"They were decent. We thought they were metal, but they turned out to be country."

"That's quite a difference if you were expecting one and got the other."

"Yeah."

She stirred the pot. He asked what she was making.

"Chili. Matt and Angie are coming over for dinner," she said.

"Really? We just saw them yesterday."

"Angie's a little down. I thought we could cheer her up."

"What's her problem?"

"Woman stuff."

He recalled what Matt told him in the car as Sam put his coffee mug in front of him. He asked if they had a good time hanging out last night. She said they did. Then she added Angie was uneasy about Matt again.

"Why?" Timothy asked.

"She didn't specify. I just think it's her old trust issues."

In this case, she was justified, given what Timothy witnessed as they left the bar. Matt didn't say a thing about it on the drive back. He was his usual self, babbling on about the band they saw, and then about another one he wanted to check out soon, with no hint he felt guilty about anything.

Timothy helped Sam work in the garden after lunch. Her phone rang. It was Angie.

"Oh, sure. I get it. Well, we'll make it another time. Don't worry. Timothy and I will eat it happily," Sam said.

She put the phone back in her pocket and bent down to pull more weeds. Timothy asked what was up. Sam said Angie wasn't feeling well and had to cancel dinner.

"She was fine yesterday," he said.

"Yeah, but not today."

When Angie was in college she had an affair with one of her professors. She was crazy about him. He wasn't crazy about her. The whole thing was over in less than a week, and Angie fell apart. She took to her bed, and said she was sick, couldn't get up, and couldn't go to class. Lavinia got to the bottom of it. Was Angie faking another illness now, and if so, was it because she found out about Matt and that girl? But how? Matt wouldn't have told her. What if the girl did something stupid and called him, and Angie overheard or snooped on his phone?

"What's the matter with you? You have the strangest look on your face," Sam said.

"Look, I have to tell you something."

"Okay."

He told her everything. Sam took off her gardening gloves and wiped the sweat out of her eyes.

"Are you *sure?*" she asked.

"Yes."

"And you didn't ask him about it?"

"No."

"Why not?"

"I don't know. I had a couple of drinks."

"Then how can you be sure of anything?"

"Because I am."

The misery which settled on Sam's face made him wish he said nothing. He wondered if she'd cry. He couldn't stand it if she did. It would be worse than the other night when she was working on her poem.

"Look, maybe there's a perfectly reasonable explanation," he said.

"Like what?"

He had no idea.

"Do you want me to talk to Matt and find out what's going on?" he asked, though the idea was appalling.

"No."

"Okay, good."

"I'll talk to him."

"Wait, no, honey, that's not a good idea."

She let it go, and they worked in the garden for over an hour. Timothy thought he'd have to take a second shower, he got so sweaty. Sam was quiet as they put their tools in the little shed they kept at the back of the yard. He said he knew how upset she was, and he understood completely because Angie was her best friend. It would be better to let Matt bring it up himself, and apologize, which he surely would.

"And what if he doesn't?" she asked.

"He'll have to. He won't want to live with a thing like that."

She crossed her arms and looked fierce. He loved her then. He really did.

"Yeah, I agree, that's probably all bull, but I still think we should stay out of it. If she says something to you, just act surprised."

"Okay."

They went in, and Timothy took a long shower. When he came out Sam was in the dining room, looking at her poetry journal. She wrote something and crossed it out. He asked if she wanted him to let her work, and she said no, she wasn't getting anywhere. She said she had a bad feeling.

"About Angie and Matt?" Timothy asked.

"Yeah."

"It'll be okay."

Sam went into the bedroom. He heard her talking on her phone. When she emerged a few minutes later, she said she called Angie to check in and see how she was doing.

"You shouldn't have called her. She might get suspicious," Timothy said.

"Chill out. I just wanted to see how she was feeling. She's running a low-grade temperature, so she's not faking if that's what you're thinking."

"Unless she's lying."

"Come on. Why would she lie about that?"

"She's not always honest about everything, believe me."

"So? No one is. You're certainly not."

"Well, I'm being honest now, and I think there's a good chance she's playing you for a fool."

Sam's face hardened. She said she hoped he wouldn't take this the wrong way, but Angie wasn't the only one who had trouble taking things at face value. Maybe it was because of his childhood, but the plain truth, as far as she could see—and she had three years of experience—was he didn't trust anyone. Which strongly suggested on some level he didn't trust *her*. He calmly denied each statement, and then gave up. He was sinking under the weight of her accusations. He said if she had such a low opinion of him, it was a good thing they weren't going to have a baby.

"Who says we're not? We haven't decided anything yet. But then, I keep waiting for you to grow up, and who knows how long *that's* going to take?" she asked.

He was on his feet, yelling at her, something he never did before. Her eyes registered shock followed by something else, quieter and more resolute.

She told him to get out.

"What?" he asked.

"I want you to leave."

"You're kicking me out? Of my own house?"

"I thought this was our house."

"That's not what I meant."

"Yes, it is."

They stood, not looking at each other. His head felt awful. And he was hungry. He wanted some of that chili, but Sam turned off the pot when they went outside.

"Don't do this," he said.

"Why not?"

Anything he said would be wrong. He looked at her as she looked at him, waiting.

"You're right. This is your house," she said and went into the bedroom. She was on her phone again. She returned with her backpack. She said she was going to his mother's place.

"Really?"

"I can't very well go to *my* mother's, can I?"

Sam's mother and her husband moved to Florida the year before to escape the upstate winters. They lived in a trailer in a shabby suburb of Miami but seemed to love it.

"No, I guess not," Timothy said. He was aware he was speaking slowly. His tongue felt thick, and his hands tingled.

Sam stood with her pack on her back as if she were going off to campus for the day and would return a few hours later, humming and asking what he wanted for dinner.

"You know where to reach me when you come to your senses," she said and left.

He went on standing for a while, not knowing what senses he was supposed to come to—about the baby, or his sister? Or even about Matt?

He went to the cabinet, took out the bourbon, and poured himself a stiff drink. It helped the pounding in his head. After the second he began to think clearly. Sam was upset about more than just the baby. All he had to do was figure out what it was and fix it. If he could.

His phone rang. It lit up with his mother's number. He let the call go to voicemail. When the icon indicated a message had been left, he listened to it.

"What the hell is going on over there? Sam showed up here in tears. That's right, in *tears*. I can't get anything out of her, and I'm not going to try. *You're* going to tell me what happened, and you're going to tell me the truth. Hear?"

"Jesus Christ," he said, and put the phone face down on the table where he sat, his free hand around his empty glass.

His real problem was that his mother spoke to him as if he were ten.

He made the bed. He thought about how to spend the rest of his day. Before he knew Matt and Angie were coming to dinner, he was going to edit some pictures he took a few weeks ago, when the skies were still gray. His heart wasn't in it, though. He already missed Sam.

He ate a bowl of cereal, then drove over to Angie's place. She met him in her pajamas and bathrobe.

"What are you doing here?" she asked. She was flushed.

"Looks like I got you out of bed. I'm sorry. Sam said you were sick. I wanted to see how you are."

"You could have called."

"Should I leave?"

"No, it's all right. Come in and make me some tea."

"Okay."

She lay down on the couch while Timothy filled the kettle with water and turned on the flame. Then he went through her cabinets until he found where she kept her tea. He asked which kind she wanted.

"Peppermint," she said.

"Okay."

He realized Matt wasn't in the house. He asked where he was.

"At the bar, where else?" Angie asked.

"He should have stayed home with you."

"He offered."

Timothy brought her the tea and put it on the coffee table. Then he sat down in the wooden rocking chair facing the couch. He looked at his phone. He turned off the ringer before getting in the car, and there were messages from Foster and each of his twin sisters. The Dugan family disaster-reporting network was up and running.

"Listen, something happened," he said.

"I know. Sam left."

"How did you find out?"

"She called me."

"When?"

"When she got in the car."

"What did she say?"

"That you're being a jerk."

"And what did you say?"

"Not much. What was I supposed to say?"

"Don't you want to know what happened?"

"Not really."

Timothy realized he was wading into dangerous territory. If he weren't careful, what he saw at the bar last night would have to come out. Angie sat up. She looked miserable. He told her to get into bed, and he could bring her tea in there if she wanted.

"Thanks," she said.

Her tabby cat, Peggy, appeared and trotted after her. When he brought in the tea, Peggy was on the end of the bed, cleaning her paws. Angie was propped up. She asked him to sit with her, so he perched next to the cat.

"Remember when we were kids and we got sick? Mom and Dad would put us all in their bed during the daytime so we could watch TV," she said.

"Yeah."

"It was kind of nice."

"Yeah."

Then Angie said there wasn't much about their childhood that was good, except for the solidarity they all developed. Timothy asked what she meant.

"We show up for each other," she said.

He wasn't sure if he agreed with that. Who showed up for him? Only Sam and she wasn't a sibling. And now she was gone.

He looked at his phone, and of course, she hadn't called. She wouldn't call. He'd have to make the first move.

"You can tell me if you want," Angie said.

"She wants a baby."

"I know."

"Everyone seems to know."

"Why would she keep it a secret?"

He said nothing. Angie brought the teacup to her lips and blew into it.

She asked if that's why she moved out—because he didn't want to be a dad.

"She didn't move out," he said.

"What would you call it?"

"She just left for a couple of days."

Angie stared him down, and he looked again at his phone. He said he had to get going. He told Angie to take care and to call if she needed anything.

The day stretched before him with nothing to do. He could finish the yardwork. Then when Sam came back, she'd be pleased. He drove out to the driving range and rented clubs and a basket of balls. He was quite the golfer back in college. Chip had a passion for the sport, too, and warmly approved. Poor Chip met his end on a golf course right there in Dunston. Got struck by lightning. As Lavinia used to say, "Zap, and that was that." Timothy didn't care to review that at the moment, however. He needed to concentrate.

He was alone on the range. He stretched to get his muscles soft and flexible. The tee slid into the ground easily. They did a good job keeping the soil moist. He took the 7-iron out of the bag and scanned the field before him, which was perfectly green and undulated toward a stand of trees. The distance markers weren't up, which the clerk mentioned. Timothy didn't mind, because he preferred to gauge his own success.

He took his stance and got a good grip on the club. It was quiet, except for the twittering of a bird in the distance. What was Sam doing? Detailing his faults to his mother? Sam wouldn't do that. She didn't run people down. He was sorry she was crying. She cried the other night, too. How long had she been that unhappy? He twisted his torso, pulled the club back, and swung. The light caught the ball as it soared, straight at first, then to the left. He hit ball after ball. They all went left. Nothing he did kept them where he wanted. He adjusted the position of his left hand and arm, lessening the force they exerted. The ball's path straightened. It was just a matter of easing up on one side. How had he never seen that before? He played so well in college, he must have known it then. He just forgot.

He practiced until he had worked up a heavy sweat. He went home and showered and put on clean clothes. His headache was back. He took some Tylenol. He hadn't looked at his phone for a while. He was sure Sam hadn't called. He should call her and tell her to come home. Better yet, he should drive over to his mother's and bring her back. But then he'd have to deal with not only his mother, but his father, unless he was working down at the bar, and Alma, who always stuck her nose in, while Sam stood silently by, waiting, watching, giving him the evil eye.

She could stay over there until hell froze over. That's just what she could do. He got into his car and drove down to Matt's bar. The place was dark and soothing, with only a few customers. It was mid-afternoon. The crowds would come later.

Matt saw him and came over to his table.

"Hey, man, what's up?" he asked and set down a coaster.

"Not much. Been out hitting balls."

"Yeah?"

"Yeah. Oh, I went by your place to see Angie. I heard she was sick."

"Just popped up overnight. Was she doing okay?"

"I put her to bed with some tea."

"Good brother."

Timothy told Matt he'd take whatever beer was good on tap. Matt said he'd be right back. At the end of the bar, seated on a stool going through some papers, was Potter. Timothy got up and went over to him.

"Hey, Pop," he said.

"Hey, what are you doing here?"

Potter's shirt was well-pressed. His hair was combed, and his eyes were clear.

"Just dropping in for a beer," Matt said.

"Where's Sam?"

"She's, well, she's at your place."

"Doing what?"

"Spending a couple of days."

Timothy gave him the summary. Potter kept looking at the stack of papers in front of him on the bar, but Timothy could see he was listening hard. He asked what set her off. Timothy told him about her wanting a baby. Potter nodded and said most women did at some point, but they didn't usually up and leave.

"Well, I did something to upset her, but I don't know what," Timothy said.

"So figure it out. And let me know how it goes."

"Okay."

Timothy returned to his table, and Matt brought out the beer. Timothy asked if he had a minute and gestured to the empty chair across from him. Matt sat down. Timothy said he wanted to know something, and Matt didn't have to answer if he didn't want to.

"Shoot," Matt said.

"That girl at the bar last night."

"What about her?"

"You kissed her goodbye."

"So?"

"Well, you kissed her on the mouth."

Matt ran his hand over the back of his wavy hair. His expression was open.

"Again, so?" he asked.

"Uh, Matt, she's not your girlfriend."

"It's no big deal."

"Okay."

"Is that why you came down today? To get the skinny on that?"

"No, of course not. I was just in the mood for a beer."

"Where's Sam?"

"Taking care of some stuff."

"Okay, well, anything else?"

"Nope."

"Beer's on the house."

"You sure?"

"Yup."

"Thanks."

"My pleasure."

Matt went back to the bar and Timothy drank his beer.

Had he just witnessed the best case of gaslighting ever? He'd known Matt a long time and always took him for a straight shooter. And since he didn't deny kissing what's-her-name on the mouth, Timothy knew he didn't imagine it.

It was a question of the guy's moral compass, Timothy thought. He might be one of those people who didn't know right from wrong. When Timothy was in college, his mother accused him of the same thing. This was just after getting busted for lifting the jacket. He knew what he did was wrong, and he did it anyway to see what happened. There were other dumb things he did that floated through his mind, but the beer helped block them out.

He debated having a second. He needed something on his stomach and asked Matt for a burger. When Matt asked if he wanted another beer, he said sure. He watched the TV mounted to the wall. The Seattle Mariners were losing badly to the Boston Red Sox. The beer showed up, followed by the burger.

Afterward, he drove to his mother's, parked, and turned off the engine. He stayed in the car. He hoped someone would see him from the window and invite him in. But there were no windows overlooking that part of the driveway, so he got out and walked around back to the kitchen door. The door was unlocked, and he went inside. Sam was on the banquette seat by the built-in table where he had breakfast every morning in high school. She looked up, and the calm expression she had before was replaced with a blend of annoyance and grief.

He held up his hand as a plea for peace.

"Come home," he said.

"Why?"

"Because that's where you belong."

She sighed and folded up the newspaper she was reading. At her elbow was her poetry journal. She was on a blank page, which meant she had an idea for something new the paper may have interrupted or given her time to cement. She could do two things at once—sometimes several things at once. It amazed him.

"Look, I'm sorry," he said.

"For what?"

He had to think. He wound back through their last exchange, which the bourbon and beer made difficult.

"Not trusting people."

She sighed again. He watched her closely. He saw no trace of the tears his mother mentioned on the phone. Where was Lavinia, anyway?

He sat down next to Sam. He told her he dropped in on Angie, made her tea, then went down to the bar to talk to Matt. He confronted him directly. Matt didn't deny anything, and the weird thing was, he seemed to think it was completely normal.

"Unbelievable," Sam said.

"For real."

Sam's shoulders relaxed. His words were helping her. She rested her head on his shoulder. He loved the nearness of her.

Lavinia came into the kitchen and stopped.

"Well, you guys made up in a hurry," she said.

"He talked to Matt," Sam said, and Timothy realized Sam told her everything. Wasn't she worried it would get back to Angie somehow? Or did they already have a plan to deal with that? Women were quick planners.

"And?" Lavinia asked. She had an empty cocktail glass in her hand.

"Just as I thought. Timothy didn't see what he thought he saw," Sam said.

She squeezed his leg.

"Well, then, don't drink so much next time. It's always good to keep a clear focus," Lavinia told him. She put the glass in the sink and left the kitchen.

"Why did you say that?" Timothy asked.

"To put an end to any further speculation."

"There wouldn't have been any speculation if you kept your mouth shut."

"Hey!"

"What I mean is, you didn't have to tell my mother everything."

"Yes, I did."

"Why?"

"Because she asked why I was upset and I wasn't going to lie."

Timothy nodded.

She looked down at the blank page of her journal. He could tell she was thinking about what she just said, and what he said in return. She was quiet, and he sat quietly, too, until he felt he'd been still long enough. He asked if she were ready to leave.

"I don't know if I should. I still have some thinking to do," she said.

"About the baby?"

"Among other things."

"Think at home."

"Well . . ."

She said it was hard because she always had so much work to do. Here, at Lavinia's, she didn't have to cook or do dishes or tidy up. It was like being on vacation.

Was that it, Timothy wondered. She needed a vacation?

He suggested it.

"I thought you didn't have any more time you could take," she said.

That was true. He took a week off in April. Every day, while she was in class, he rambled around the snowy countryside with his camera, taking a few shots, mostly of barns.

"I don't mind not getting paid. It's okay," he said.

"Where would we go?"

They'd never gone anywhere together. He suggested they could visit his sisters in Manhattan.

"You know I hate the city," she said.

That, too, was true.

"How about Maine?" he asked.

"Okay."

He said they could rent a cabin on a lake unless she wanted to hang out on the beach. She said the beach might be fun, but wouldn't the water be too cold to swim in? He thought it would. She said a lake would be too cold, too, but it sounded so peaceful. Not that a beach *wasn't* peaceful, that's not what she meant.

"I know," he said.

She said she promised Lavinia she'd stay for dinner.

"Do you have to?" he asked.

"I said I would."

"Okay."

"Join us, if you want."

"I'll skip it if you don't mind."

Sam looked relieved, and he knew they'd have another heart-to-heart, probably about him.

"I'll come home after," she said.

"Promise?"

"Of course."

He kissed her. She kissed him back.

When he returned to his car he sat for a while before turning on the engine. Then he drove himself home, where he heated the chili and let it simmer for a long time before having a heaping bowl of it. He drank and read his book. Of course, he already knew how the Spaniards had totally shafted the Incas, but it still made him mad as hell. They sounded like cool people, offing their kids notwithstanding.

The light dimmed and the sky was dark. Sam hadn't returned. That must be some heavy talk she and his mother were having. He went into the kitchen to get himself another drink and discovered the bottle was empty. He couldn't possibly have had it all! But there it was, empty and soulless, sitting on the counter by his dirty dishes. Sam wouldn't want to deal with his mess in the morning, so he rinsed everything and opened the dishwasher. The dishes in it were clean. He was getting tired and didn't want to put them away.

When he woke in the morning, he saw he overslept. Then he realized Sam hadn't come home. He fumbled for his phone and found a message from her saying she stayed up late at Lavinia's and thought it would be easier to stay over there.

Jesus Christ, he thought. They lived in the same damn neighborhood. What was it, a little over a mile? And that was too far to drive? She didn't want to come home, that was it. She was sticking it to him for . . . he didn't even know, at that point.

When he got to work Jiao and Jimmy were manning the store. Jiao wore a different nose ring. He thought after you got something pierced, you were supposed to leave it alone, not take things in and out, so it could heal. He was going to ask her about it when he realized she and Jimmy were looking at him crossly. He said he had car trouble and knew he should have called.

"That old Mercedes is more of a pain than it's worth," he said, cheerfully.

Sue was dressing some child-sized mannequins in the back. She was pale. He told her if she still weren't feeling well, she should just go back home.

"Can't. No more sick days this month," she said. She coughed without covering her mouth.

She got one mannequin into a sleeveless pink top and white shorts. He helped her wrestle the other one into a plaid jumper. The plastic legs felt cold and greasy. He asked her when they were last washed.

"What, the mannequins? I have no idea. Are you *supposed* to wash them?"

"When they feel like this, you do."

"Okay."

She removed the outfits. He carried the two mannequins into the breakroom and filled the sink with water. There was a bottle of dish soap and a sponge. He tried to stand one mannequin in the sink and it wouldn't balance on its own, so he held it with one hand and tried to wash it with the other. That was too difficult, so he unscrewed the legs and washed them one at a time. He dried them with a paper towel and pressed the right leg into the hole he pulled it out of. It wouldn't go in, no matter how he twisted and turned it.

"God damn it!"

Jiao appeared.

"What's wrong, Boss?" she asked even though Timothy said before he didn't like being called that. He explained the situation. Jiao told him to press on one side of the leg, and when he did, it slid into where it was supposed to go just fine. She offered to finish the job for him, and he told her to go back to the sales floor. He'd manage.

As he was putting the second mannequin back together, Jiao returned and said someone was on the floor asking for him. He dried his hands and tucked in his shirt. He arranged his face into a pleasant, helpful expression, and went out.

He recognized him at once. Charlie Harcourt, from his Kappa Alpha days, wearing a suit and high-end loafers.

"Brother!" Timothy boomed with a cheer he didn't feel.

"Dugan!"

They shook hands, then banged each other on the back. Harcourt had aged. There were fine lines around his eyes and a few gray hairs among the thick red wavy ones.

"How did you know I worked here?" Timothy asked.

"I saw you in here the other day. I'd have stopped in then, but I was late for a meeting."

"So, you're back in Dunston."

"Never left. Couldn't tear myself away, I guess."

"You have time for coffee?"

"Absolutely."

Timothy told Jiao he was stepping out for a few minutes. He and Harcourt wandered into the mall. Harcourt took up a lot of space when he walked as if the whole place belonged to him. Timothy recalled his family had money.

"How are you staying busy?" Timothy asked.

"This and that. Real estate, mostly. I'm putting up a development over in Dryden."

"Nice!"

"I need a partner if you're interested."

"Seriously?"

"Why not? I remember you always had a good head for figures."

"Yeah, my stepfather was always on me about how much of his money I was spending, so I learned how to keep track. That seemed to calm him down a little," Timothy said.

"The guy that got struck by lightning?"

"The very same."

"Weird as hell."

They got in line for the coffee. When their turn came, Harcourt paid for both of them, although Timothy already had his credit card in his hand. He thought about going into business with Harcourt. This might be what he needed to move forward with his life, a good solid business opportunity.

They took a table and waited for the barista to bring them their order. Harcourt's hands were on the table. He had the same pinky ring he wore in school, a sapphire set in gold. Timothy remembered him sliding it off and throwing it on the poker table when he ran out of cash to bet. No one could agree on a fair value for the ring, so Harcourt had to fold.

"You look well," Harcourt said.

"Hungover as hell."

"Same old Dugan."

The barista put down the cups, each decorated with an elegant swirl of steamed milk. When she left, Harcourt said there was something else he wanted to talk to him about.

"Okay," Timothy said.

"It's sort of a delicate matter."

"Shoot."

"Do you remember that girl, Melissa? Junior year?"

Timothy stopped stirring his coffee.

"Sure," he said.

"I ran into her the other day."

"Yeah?"

Harcourt said he was just walking down the Commons and there she was, looking in a store window with her kid.

"She has a kid? Who'd she marry?" Timothy asked.

"Nobody."

"Oh. Oops."

Harcourt sipped his coffee. "The kid's yours."

Timothy set his cup down in the saucer and leaned back to get a better look at Harcourt.

"No way," he said.

"I'm just telling you what she told me."

"And you believed her?"

"Dugan, the kid looks just like you."

"Boy, I presume?"

"Yup."

Timothy told him to hold on a second. Why had he never heard from Melissa himself, if this were true? They only slept together once, in any case.

"Yeah, well, it only takes one time," Harcourt said.

"This isn't funny."

"I'm not laughing, and no, it's not."

Timothy stood up to leave and Harcourt asked him to give him just another minute. Timothy sat down.

"Look, she's between jobs and it's a little tough at the moment," Harcourt said.

"Sounds like she was making up a sob story so you'd give her money."

"Maybe. I gave it to her anyway."

"Jesus."

"It's okay. I'm not going to ask you to pay me back."

"What the hell? You don't even know if the kid's really mine!"

"Take a DNA test."

"Are you *nuts?*"

"Then you'll know."

Harcourt sipped his coffee and assumed a bland, disinterested air, as if having done his duty, he could just sit back and savor the drip of the day, but Timothy knew him well enough to know he was simply opening a space for whatever came next.

Melissa.

God, what a train wreck.

It seemed so innocent at the time. His frat brothers dared him to get involved with her because she ran a group on campus that preached abstinence. He didn't think anyone would get hurt. She was already hurt, he discovered, by getting raped by her father's business partner. That whole thing messed her up so badly she started the group. She said she knew, in the beginning, that she was just looking for some kind of safe harbor, but then it began to make sense. You don't have sex with people, and bad things can't happen. Later, after they dated a little while, she said she'd have been better off forming a group to spotlight the horrors of rape, but there were plenty of those around. Timothy fell in love with her, or so he thought. Those feelings were not reciprocated. After their one-night stand, she stopped answering his calls, and he learned she left school and went home to Buffalo. He was depressed about it for a long time.

Harcourt was looking at him.

"You can give her my number," Timothy said.

"Which is?"

Timothy recited the digits and Harcourt tapped them into his phone. Then he slid the phone into the inner pocket of his jacket. He talked about the development he was working on, made up of three and four-bedroom homes on quarter-acre lots. A little cookie-cutter, he said, but they were mixing up styles and landscaping. Permits had become a problem in some cases. Something was going on down at the county zoning office he was trying to unravel. The partner he was looking for would keep track of interested buyers and get them to the closing table. Did that sound interesting?

"It does," Timothy said. He hadn't had any of his coffee and thought it was cold.

"You could drive out to the construction office and meet my contractor."

"Sure."

Harcourt gave him the address. He said he hoped Timothy didn't mind his mentioning Melissa. He wanted to catch up with him, anyway and hoped they'd get together again soon, whether or not they ended up working together.

They stood and shook hands. Timothy watched Harcourt walk away through the mall, then went back to the store and dressed the mannequins, whose plastic limbs still felt dirty.

Chapter Four

Sam had the whole kitchen turned upside down. She said when she walked in that morning, she realized it needed a good cleaning. The cabinets were empty, and the dishes, glassware, pots, and pans lined the countertops and the dining room table. She was in her old denim overalls, which meant she'd be at it for hours. He was hungry and wondered about dinner.

"Did you have a good talk with my mother?" he asked.

With her back to him and one arm deep in an upper cabinet, she said, "Yeah. Though mostly she just wanted to talk about your dad."

"Is she having second thoughts?"

"I don't think so."

"Well, I'm glad you're home." He kissed her on the cheek. She stopped scrubbing for a moment and resumed.

She asked how his day was. He told her about washing the mannequins. She said she heard from Angie that she was still under the weather but improving.

"That's good," he said.

He sat on one of the counter stools and thought about Harcourt. He was a smug prick and the kind of guy that always told other people what to think. He once treated Timothy to a grueling lecture about one of their frat brothers, Jeremy something, who adopted most of Timothy's attitudes about school (cynical) and women (also cynical), and drinking (with serious intent.) Timothy couldn't stand the guy, and Harcourt said he should try to be a good role model, and realize that imitation was the sincerest form of flattery. Another time, when Timothy complained about getting a C on some paper he dashed off the day before it was due, Harcourt told him to go in and demand to be given a C+. He said it was important to be able to persuade people to do things they didn't want to do—he had that from his old man, himself. Timothy told Harcourt he was a pompous ass. Harcourt was sullen for days, then erupted over a game of pool. He accused Timothy of cheating, which Timothy said was impossible since Harcourt watched every move he called, but Harcourt persisted. They fought, and Timothy gave him a black eye. After that, they were close friends. Timothy learned all about Harcourt's awful family—his older brother, Chad, who worked for a congressman, and his father, who owned a small pharmaceutical company. Sometimes Harcourt got drunk and broke down crying about what rotten bastards they both were. Timothy thought it would be hard to live like that, wanting approval from people who hated you. Timothy nursed him through a terrible break-up with a girl he was mad about; Harcourt let Timothy ramble on and on about Melissa when she didn't want to see him again. But when school ended, their friendship didn't continue. At the time he wondered about it and thought they might not have been as close as he assumed, but that afternoon, having coffee, he felt that friendship again, though the circumstances were bizarre.

Sam finished the cabinets and took the empty stool next to him.

"I'm beat," she said.

"Yeah, you've been working hard."

"As my mother used to say, it's good to stay busy when the mind is full."

"And what is your mind full of?"

She looked at him. "You know perfectly well."

"Sure."

But he wasn't sure. It could be about Matt, the baby thing, or even that poetry reading. He asked if she thought any more about going on vacation.

"I choose a lake," she said.

"Excellent. Let me jump online and see what's available."

"Are you hungry?"

"A little."

"I can reheat the chili."

"Let's order Chinese. If that's okay."

"Might be easier. I still have to put the kitchen back together."

"You want help?"

"Nah, I got it."

He went into the spare room and used the computer to search for vacation cabins on lakes in Maine. The pictures made him wistful for something he couldn't name, not necessarily the rustic beauty of nature, which Dunston had plenty of, but for the cozy darkness offered by the thick stands of pine trees. One place had cabins set far apart from one another, which Timothy liked a lot. They could sit on the porch and watch the surface of the water. It would be relaxing. They would chill and become friends again, with all that time to talk, or not talk.

Sam set the table. Over kung pao chicken Timothy laid out the options. The place he was leaning toward was Moosehead Lake. Out in the middle of nowhere. No one to bother them. Sam asked what they would do about food. He said the cabin had a small kitchen. It even came with a set of dishes, and some pots and pans.

Sam pointed her chopsticks at Timothy.

"Who's going to cook?" she asked.

"Well, I will."

"Right."

"I will."

"You can't even boil water."

"Come on. I do better than that."

"When was the last time you made me anything to eat?"

He thought. She was sick last year. He made her soup. When he said so, she reminded him all he did was empty a can into a pan and heat it. That was hardly cooking.

"Well, then we'll do take-out," he said.

"You said this place was in the middle of nowhere. Where are we going to get take-out?"

He stabbed a piece of chicken with his chopsticks.

"We'll buy a bunch of bread and cold cuts. We'll live on sandwiches," he said.

"Even for breakfast?"

"We'll find a diner—there must be one—and we'll have breakfast there."

"And get to know the locals."

"We'll wear baseball caps."

"And fleece vests."

"And lose our 'r's."

They laughed. He asked if she were finished. She said she was. He cleared their plates, rinsed them, and put them in the dishwasher.

"Remember that guy?" he asked.

"What guy?"

"That guy in the diner downtown. Didn't he say he was from Maine?"

"New Hampshire."

"I'm sure it was Maine."

Sam shook her head. She had her poetry journal out. Timothy wasn't aware she went to get it.

"What about him?" she asked.

"He was a character."

"Yeah."

He saw her remembering.

They were out for a drive last winter, even though it was freezing. Sam had a bad day in class or got a bad grade, or someone didn't like the poem she shared in seminar. No, it was about her mother, that was it. She—Flora—called again to ask for money. Sam had a healthy stash from what her father invested for her when she was born and had no plans to share. She might have if her mother hadn't lied. Flora's story was her father wanted nothing to do with her, when in fact, he tried to be in her life and Flora prevented it. Sam confronted Flora when she learned the truth from her father but didn't tell her about the money. How Flora knew she had it, all the way down in Florida, was nothing short of a miracle. She must have begged extra hard because after the call, Sam broke down crying and Timothy could see he had to get her out of there. He threw her in the car and they drove way out in the country until she calmed down. She said she never wanted to see her mother again. Timothy thought it was a harsh statement, but he understood.

On the way back into town Sam said she was hungry. They went to Moe's, a diner downtown. Timothy was a regular there back in college, usually in the wee hours after a night of hard drinking. It was a Tuesday and slow. They were the only ones in the place until that guy from Maine came in. He sat down at the counter next to them and got chatty. Timothy didn't answer his casual remarks about the weather, but Sam did. Why did she take the bait? She was like that though, wasn't she? Always willing to give someone a try.

This guy went on and on about being there to visit his daughter, only she moved and he lost her address. Timothy thought he was about to get a hard-luck story followed by a plea for a couple of bucks. Sam was drawn in. Had he called his daughter? Of course, that was the first thing he tried. Did he leave a message? Yup. Did he have her former address? He did. Well, if she had roommates, he could go over there and ask them. Timothy kept glancing at her to suggest she disengage, but she kept going. She told him about moving out to LA years before, not telling her mother her new address on purpose, and how her mother eventually tracked her down because Sam happened to mention the name of the motel where she worked as a maid. Oh, did this guy know where his daughter worked? At that point, the guy's phone rang and it was his daughter, telling him how to find her new house.

He paid his bill and left, and Sam said he was such a nice guy.

But when did he say mentioned he was from Maine? Timothy asked her that now.

"New Hampshire. And when I asked, remember?" she asked.

"You weren't sitting next to him, I was."

"So?"

"So, that's why you don't remember."

"Where I was sitting has nothing to do with it."

"It doesn't matter."

She stared at her journal, then picked up her pencil. Timothy went out back and sat on the porch. The yard waste container was where they left it the other day. He could put it in the garage. He was surprised Sam didn't do it. She was a tidy person.

Harcourt was a jerk, dumping that news on him like that. It just didn't make any sense that Melissa kept a child from him all this time. She'd have needed money before then and come looking for it. Her pride stopped her. She was a proud person, yet she also needed love. Timothy tried to give it to her. She wouldn't accept it. He wished now he asked Harcourt for her number, but if he had it and called, what the hell would he possibly say? And what was he going to say to Sam?

Nothing.

Not until he learned the truth about that kid.

The light dropped, and Timothy went on sitting. He sent a text message to each of his sisters in New York, saying everything was fine now with Sam. Then he texted Angie to ask if she were feeling better.

Yeah, some, she wrote back immediately. Then, *How are things over there?*

They're cool, he typed back.

Through the open screen door, he heard Sam moving around. She was looking for something in the kitchen. It was odd she didn't know where it was. She knew where everything was. He heard the water run. She must be making tea. Yeah, that was it. A few minutes later she appeared with a steaming mug that smelled like peppermint. She sat in the chair next to his.

"Listen, I've been thinking," she said.

"Yeah?"

"I want you to get some counseling. Your mother and I talked about it. She'll pay for it."

"Wait a minute. I don't need counseling."

She blew into the cup.

"You're super stressed out all the time, and you drink too much," she said.

"Who says?"

"You know it's true."

"Sam, give me a break. I did all that before."

"Doesn't mean you don't need another round."

His mother was behind it the first time, too. This was in college when his drinking got out of hand. Chip said he wasn't going to pay for another semester unless he pulled his GPA up. Timothy told them both to go to hell. He jumped in his car, a brand-new Buick Chip thought was an appropriate gift for a booze-soaked twenty-year-old, and took off. He went over to Boston and stayed in a lavish hotel suite, not drinking as much as he planned, just reveling in being alone where he didn't know anyone. With Chip's credit card he ate well, bought some gorgeous hand-made Italian boots, wandered around Cambridge and Harvard Square, and began to imagine a new life for himself. Chip got wise and canceled the card. Timothy couldn't pay his hotel bill. He climbed down the fire escape with his new purchases—he picked up some books, too—went to the garage where his car was parked, and left. He took his time getting back to Dunston. He stayed in cheap places all around New England, using his own money he withdrew from an ATM. Those were good days, sober days, where things were proportionate and logical. The books he bought were all histories of other civilizations. The one on ancient Rome was captivating. Knowing the past had been lived by people just like him made him see everything was temporary.

When he got home, Chip took away his car keys. Timothy was ordered to move out of the frat and back into the house so his behavior could be monitored. That was all Chip's idea, with the understanding that Lavinia would act as supervisor, a role she had no interest in performing. Her argument, which was a good one, was that she watched out for Potter for the better part of twenty years and that was enough. She told Timothy to get his act together, and if he couldn't, he had to talk to a therapist. Cleverly (or so he thought) he agreed if they would return his car and credit card, and let him move back to the frat. He was told he had to prove himself, first. He accepted their terms. He would have accepted anything just to get away from them.

Her name was Audrey Moss, and she was easily in her seventies. Lavinia played her hand. She felt Timothy had a bad attitude toward the opposite sex. Privately, he thought it was no wonder, given how fierce both she and Angie were. His twin sisters . . . well, they weren't fierce, but spoiled, devious, given to wild flights of fancy.

Dr. Moss was as shriveled as a prune, but her eyes were open and kind. He told her he knew he was a bad person and was trying to learn how to live with that. She asked if he were a bad person or just did bad things. He said he did bad things. When she asked why he said to feel safe.

"Safe from what?" she asked.

"Pain."

She regarded him at length. If he stood up and walked out, would she say anything? Do anything? He stayed.

She asked him what hurt and how long it had been going on, like a doctor poking his stomach.

Over the next weeks and months, he discovered putting up a wall against his father to protect himself from the constant disappointment of his alcoholism required a degree of emotional detachment that didn't come naturally to a child. He grew to doubt his ability to love and meaningfully connect. Relationships were transactional.

He drank less and applied himself in school. His grades went up, the car was returned, and so was his generous allowance. He moved back to the frat. He thought his time with Dr. Moss, while not life-changing, let him refocus.

Then the brothers dared him to seduce Melissa. He still didn't understand why he agreed. He worked so hard to persuade himself he could be open and honest with someone, and what did he do? Make up a huge lie about wanting to join her stupid abstinence group.

And since then? It seemed as if he just drifted, going along the path of least resistance. What was wrong with that, anyway?

"Let me ask you something," he said to Sam.

"Okay."

"How do you see me?"

"As a man who doesn't know how to be happy."

"I'm happy with you."

She looked at him probingly. "You used to be, I think."

She set her mug on the porch and gazed into the garden and the thinning light.

"Do you think I don't love you? Is that it?" he asked.

She said nothing.

"No, that's not it," she said, at last.

"I'll find a therapist if you want. If you think it's important."

She lifted her cup and held it with both hands as if she enjoyed the warmth it gave. After a moment she set it back on the porch. He stared at their hydrangea bush. He hated it. The flowers reminded him of old ladies. He told Sam once he thought they should get rid of it. She said no, it was beautiful.

She cleared her throat. He wondered if she'd cry. Her eyes stayed dry.

"Tell me what the problem is," he said.

"I just sometimes wonder . . ."

"What?"

"If I've changed."

"I don't think you have."

"I think I have."

"Okay. Do you think I've changed?" he asked.

"I don't know."

"People are supposed to change a little over time, aren't they?"

"Well, if they do, they're supposed to realize it and go from there."

"And where do you think we should go from here?"

"Forward, if we can."

"Together?"

She was quiet.

"Yes, together," she said.

She lifted the tea again. This time she tasted it. She gave up using sugar, and from the face she made, she regretted it.

He said he read an article once about how hard it was to keep relationships fresh—that sense of newness people enjoy in the beginning. She asked where he found it, the article. He said he didn't remember, in a magazine, probably at the dentist's office. Anyway, it said it was good to share something new about yourself, because your partner might think they knew everything there was to know, and that was never true, right?

"I suppose," she said.

She drank her tea. The light dropped further and at the back of the yard, some fireflies blinked on and off like fragments of a larger, more beautiful idea, though by themselves they were beautiful. He always loved fireflies, if not the season they came with. He wondered what it was about summer he didn't like. School let out and he was stuck at home with his brother and sisters, hiding out from Angie's sharp tongue and his father's drunken stumbles. He waited every day for his mother to return from work. She was tired and often bad-tempered, but her presence always calmed him because she was competent and reliable. It was the heat that was hard on him. , though he didn't usually feel it. Or the light, but again, he seldom noticed.

No, it was summer's air of expectation, the promise that things would ease and be pleasant when they never were.

"I hate summer," he said.

She looked at him. "I know."

"How?"

"You're always restless in the summer. You're much easier to live with when it's cold."

"Oh."

She asked him if that were the thing he chose to share about himself. He said it was.

"Does it still count if I already knew?" she asked.

"Good question."

"Well, we can decide that later."

"Okay. Now, it's your turn."

She tied her hair into a knot, something she did when she wanted to concentrate.

She said when she was about ten or eleven her family sent her to camp.

"Yeah?"

The flash in her eyes asked him to please let her finish.

Anyway, they never had any money lying around so they must have scrounged a long time for it. It was the summer when she and her grandmother fought almost daily—he remembered she and her mother lived with them, right?

"Yup."

Sam's mother thought it best to get her out of the house for a while, to give things a chance to settle down, though the only thing that had to settle down was her grandmother's wicked temper. Anyway, she was happy to go, though her duffle bag was crazy heavy.

"I don't even remember what was in it. A sleeping bag, but I don't know what else," she said.

"Right."

The camp was on the lake somewhere, and everyone went swimming every afternoon, although the water was really cold. Sam couldn't swim well, so she stayed where it was shallow and just sort of paddled here and there until the lifeguard blew her whistle to say it was time to get out.

One of the other campers was learning disabled and the girls made fun of her. Sam stood up for this girl, and because she was big and didn't mind taking a swing at someone, her protection was respected. The girl, Sara-Beth, kept going too far out in the lake and getting into trouble when the water got deep. She thrashed around and cried out until someone swam out and hauled her back to safety. Finally, the counselors decided she couldn't be allowed in the lake at all unless someone watched her the whole time. Sam volunteered. And for a while, Sara-Beth did as Sam asked, she stayed close, and everything was hunky-dory. But then one day Sam got distracted by something, an argument between two girls nearby, and she was drawn into their quarrel, not picking sides, just waiting to see who would win. And of course, Sara-Beth moseyed on into the lake further and further and got in trouble. She called and called for Sam and Sam tried to get to her but couldn't. The lifeguard charged into the lake and fished Sara-Beth out. Sara-Beth was fine, no harm done, but Sam felt awful for letting her down.

"That's quite a story," Timothy said.

The knot in Sam's hair had loosened while she talked, and stray strands framed her face.

"I'm sure you think it's a little obvious," she said.

"How?"

"That my maternal instincts were triggered and never quit."

"I don't think that at all."

"Okay."

The light around them was gone, and a gibbous moon was visible over the trees. The fireflies were easy to see in the blackness of the yard.

"Do we feel closer now?" he asked.

"I don't know."

Later, after they made love the way they used to in the old days, he fell into a deep sleep. When he woke Sam was crying softly into her pillow. He didn't know if he should comfort her or pretend he didn't hear. Before he could decide, he fell back asleep.

Chapter Five

In the morning Sam apologized. She said she didn't know what was wrong with her lately. She was at the dining room table in the oversized T-shirt she wore to bed. On her feet were a pair of fuzzy slippers in a hot shade of pink. For someone who didn't go in for girly things, those slippers were a bit much.

Timothy kissed the top of her head and realized she hadn't washed her hair for a couple of days. That wasn't like her. He poured her a cup of coffee, then one for himself, and joined her. The flowers she put in a vase over the weekend were wilting in greenish water. Last summer, after classes ended, she went through the same thing, a period of not knowing how to fill her days. Eventually, she found a group of women online to go walking with. All of them were much older, and she became a quick favorite. She was fussed over and treated like a daughter. He didn't know if she were interested in doing something like that again. He reminded her about their trip over to Maine.

"Oh, I don't think we should go," she said.

"What? Why not?"

"I just don't feel like it right now."

"You're just in a slump. Once we hit the road, you'll pull out of it."

She met his eye, but he could see her mind was far away. He thought of calling in sick, spending the day with her, and taking her to a movie. When he suggested it, she said he shouldn't, she was fine, she was just off to a slow start.

She asked what he felt like having for dinner.

"Why don't we go out?" he asked.

"Oh, that's a nice idea! What do you feel like?"

"How about that new Italian place near campus?"

"Should I make a reservation?"

"Sure!"

She got up and put a piece of toast in the toaster. He said he'd call her later.

"Okay," she said.

On the way to work, Harcourt called. He wanted to know if Timothy were free for lunch to talk more about his offer.

"Man, you didn't give me a lot of time to think it over," Timothy said.

"The market's going to heat up come fall, and I want my new guy in place."

"Pushy."

"Realistic."

Timothy rolled to a stop. A police car cruised past, but Timothy's phone was properly placed in the hands-free holder mounted to his dashboard. He drove on.

He told Harcourt he'd be at his office around one. Then he asked if he heard from Melissa.

"Not a peep," Harcourt said.

"I've been wondering if I should call her and get to the bottom of this."

"Up to you. I have her number."

"I'll let you know at lunch."

"Cool."

There were an unusually large number of shoppers throughout the morning, and Timothy wondered if he should cancel with Harcourt. Then he thought, to hell with that. With luck, he'd be leaving this lousy job soon. It was odd to think about, given how long he worked there. Sam liked to say the universe had a way of shifting things when you least expected it, and now was one of those times. He asked Sue if she unpacked the new arrivals, and she winked at him and said she had. He said he was glad to see she was feeling better. Then Jiao showed up in jeans and a T-shirt that said, Do Me Now.

"What are you doing? You can't wear that," Timothy said. Jimmy laughed. Sue shook her head. Jiao pulled another T-shirt out of her purse and said she'd go change. She just wanted to see what Timothy would say about the other one.

"Ha, ha," he said.

"She digs you, man," Jimmy said when she went into the dressing room.

"Get out."

"It's true."

Timothy looked to see where Sue was and if she overheard. She was in the men's section, folding blue jeans and stacking them in the display cubicles. He wondered what it would be like to sleep with her. No better than it ever was with Sam. Then there'd be all that guilt to deal with, not to mention the threat of a jealous husband on the loose. And as to Jiao, he still had no interest there, despite Jimmy's remark. He told everyone he was taking a long lunch and to behave themselves while he was out.

Harcourt's office was a trailer set back on the edge of a dirt lot. On the hill behind it was a two-story house with a bay window on either side of the front door, and three smaller windows up. There were several homes in various stages of completion and a backhoe leveling a patch of ground. Timothy didn't know the area had grown so much. When he was a kid there was nothing out here.

Harcourt was wearing a sports shirt and khaki slacks. His face was tense as he talked into his phone. Another man was in the trailer at a second desk, looking at architectural plans. He looked at Timothy, and Timothy pointed to Harcourt, and the man went back to what he was doing. Harcourt swung around in his chair and held up his finger to say he'd be off the phone in another minute. There was a couch across from Harcourt's desk, and Timothy sat down on it. The place had a cozy feel. He thought it would be nice in the winter, with the snow raging outside. If the electric baseboard radiators didn't quite do the job, you could always put in a wood stove.

"I told you we can't," Harcourt said and hung up.

He stood up and came out from behind the desk.

"Let me introduce you to my contractor, Jack," Harcourt said, and Timothy stood up, too. Jack rolled up his plans and shook Timothy's hand.

"An old frat brother," Harcourt said.

"Ah," Jack said. Timothy got the feeling from Jack's hurried manner that he wasn't impressed with Harcourt. He was older, probably in his fifties, and might think Harcourt was too young to be his boss. Harcourt asked Timothy if he wanted to take a look around at the houses they were building.

"Sound great!"

They went outside and got into a golf cart parked in the shade of the only tree standing nearby.

"Where did you get this baby?" Timothy asked.

"Saw an ad in the paper."

They got in and Harcourt started the engine. He said it needed a minute to warm up.

"When did you decide to get into the home building business?" Timothy asked.

"Last year."

"What were you doing before?"

"I was in business with my wife."

"Wife."

"Elena. We're divorced. Guess I couldn't hack married life."

"Wow, sorry to hear that, man."

"Thanks."

Harcourt steered the cart up a dirt road. It strained but took the incline. The land was divided into lots, marked with stakes. The stakes were tied with pink plastic ribbons that fluttered in the breeze. Some lots had a mature elm tree, most were bare. The sun was high, and Timothy was grateful for the cart's awning.

They passed the house Timothy saw when he arrived. Harcourt said it was the model home. A construction crew was installing insulation on the next house, and across the road, two guys used staple guns to install plywood.

Timothy asked Harcourt where he met his wife.

"In the flower shop she owned. On the Commons."

"And what brought you into a place like that?"

"She did. If you saw her through the window, you'd have gone in, too."

The dirt road continued to climb. On their right, the skeleton of another house stood, the window cut-outs like blind eyes trying to find the sun. The insistent beeping of the backhoe behind them made conversation impossible for a few minutes.

"What was she like? If you don't mind talking about it, that is," Timothy asked, when it was quiet.

"She had a good head for business and wanted to get ahead. We were on the same page there. Then I mentioned having kids one day. She was dead set against that. There were other problems, of course, but that was the biggest."

The dirt road ended at a higher field that wasn't staked. Harcourt turned off the cart and they got out. Because of the steady climb, they had a splendid view of the lake. Harcourt said the homes up here would sit on bigger lots. Jack thought they should all be Colonial style, but Harcourt preferred Craftsman. What did Timothy think?

"My mother's house is a Colonial. Frankly, I think it's ugly. Craftsman's better," he said.

"Totally."

They strolled across the field. Timothy asked Harcourt what his plans were for landscaping.

"Haven't nailed that down, yet," Harcourt said.

"My girlfriend is great with plants. At least, she redid our backyard. A small space, but she made it shine. I could talk to her, get her input."

Harcourt nodded. His mind was elsewhere.

Timothy asked how much interest there was in the properties so far.

"A fair amount. People like the idea of new construction," Harcourt said. "But Jack tends to put clients off. He's a little rough around the edges, as you saw."

"My dad got involved in his ex-wife's remodeling company for the same reason. She was rough, too."

"What's he do now?"

"Works in a bar he invested in."

Timothy could see Harcourt remembering him talking about Potter back in college.

"He cleaned up his act a lot," Timothy said. Then he asked what the job would pay.

"You take some of the profits. Say, twenty percent."

"And what about you and Jack?"

"Jack gets fifteen percent. I get thirty. The rest goes back into the company."

"Sounds reasonable."

Timothy thought about leaving the GAP. He figured he'd been there long enough. He said he should talk it over with Sam, but would probably accept. Harcourt shook his hand and asked if he wanted to get something to eat.

"Yeah, I'm starved."

They got back in the golf cart and made their way down the hill. Harcourt asked whose car he wanted to take. Timothy said he preferred to take his.

The place they always went to in college was perfect for the growing sense of nostalgia they both felt. Sam and Timothy used to go often when they first got together, but then Sam didn't like the varsity atmosphere. They sat in the back and talked about old times. Harcourt got expansive after the first beer, and so did Timothy.

"About Melissa," Timothy said.

"Yeah?"

"I don't think I should call her."

"As I say, that's totally up to you."

"If she calls me, fine."

They ate their burgers and had another round. Harcourt grew quiet, and Timothy worried that talking about his ex-wife might have upset him. Then he lightened up. He said again he was sorry he didn't stay in touch after school. There'd been just so much going on.

Timothy asked what they did with the flower shop. Harcourt said they sold it when they split up. Last he heard, the new owner was turning it into a clothing boutique. He didn't want a flower shop at all, just a conveniently located space on the Commons.

"Makes sense," Timothy said. He was getting drunk. He thought that was okay because he decided not to go back to work that day. He asked Harcourt when he could start working for him—or with him. Harcourt said whenever was fine, but they needed one more meeting to talk about financial specifics. Maintaining a big cash reserve against shortfalls and losses was crucial.

"Do you have a good accountant?" Timothy asked

"Yeah. She's good."

"Long as she's honest."

"She's honest. Far as I can tell."

Being in business was interesting, Harcourt said. You learned how to read people and get a sense of what they wanted even if they didn't know it themselves.

"My stepfather used to say that," Timothy said.

"What was he like?"

"Oh, I don't know. He was a good guy. I think my mother drove him nuts."

Timothy talked about moving into Chip's huge house and how strange it felt to finally have a room of his own. Chip tried to take him under his wing, which meant being taught how to play golf, tie a tie, and even mix cocktails.

"So he's the reason you love to drink so much," Harcourt said and signaled the server for another round.

"Nah. If I got it from anyone, it was my dad."

They discussed their former frat brothers and wondered how they were doing. One became a dog breeder; another flunked out of medical school. Harcourt learned these things at their tenth reunion, which Timothy didn't attend. It had been twelve years since he graduated from college, and thirteen since the fiasco with Melissa. He couldn't believe so much time had gone by.

Hours passed. Other customers came and went. The light through the dirty windows that looked out onto the sidewalk fell. Harcourt said he should be getting back.

Timothy looked at his watch. It was after six. What the hell? He hadn't lost track of time like that for a while. Oh, well. They needed to catch up.

Out on the street, Harcourt asked if Timothy were sober enough to drive.

"No, but I'll make it. I always do."

"Good man."

Once behind the wheel, Timothy's mind cleared, and focusing on driving was a breeze. He ferried Harcourt back to the construction office. Then he asked if *he* could make it home all right.

"Never better," Harcourt said. They agreed to be in touch soon.

The light on the lake was lovely, and Timothy's spirits soared. Here was the way forward he was looking for. Man, life was good. Without even asking, he found the answer.

Sam was in the kitchen, talking on her phone. She told whomever it was she'd get back to them.

"Where the hell have you been?" she asked. She was flushed and had been crying. There were dirty dishes in the sink. Unfolded laundry lined the counter.

"I had lunch with Harcourt. To talk about the job," he said.

"Who's Harcourt? What job?"

He realized he hadn't told her anything. He started to and she cut him off.

"Lunch? It's almost seven o'clock, for god's sake," she said.

"We lost track of time. You know, catching up."

He got himself a glass of water. He could feel the mother of all headaches coming on.

"We were supposed to go out to dinner, remember? I made a reservation. I called you and you didn't pick up. I've been calling all afternoon. I even called the store. They said you left and didn't come back."

He sat down at the counter and stared at a pile of his clean boxers.

"I'm sorry," he said. He finished the glass of water and wanted a second.

"Sorry? I've been worried sick. I've been calling everyone. They probably all think you're dead."

"Sam."

She put her phone on the counter and walked into the yard. He saw her standing there, arms crossed, looking at the bushes.

He pulled his phone out of his pocket. Sure enough, the ringer was off and there were a million texts and voice messages. Most were from Sam. A lot were from Angie and Potter. Lavinia only called once. The twins each called twice, and Foster valiantly left four texts:

Hey, Sam's worried, can you call her?

Hey, me again, what are you doing? Call Sam.

Guess who? Listen, this is getting totally weird. Everyone's flipping out.

Are you out getting loaded?

Timothy got himself another glass of water and went into the yard to join Sam.

"We can still go to dinner now if you want," he said.

She turned and looked at him. "You're in no shape for that. How much did you have to drink, anyway? And you shouldn't be driving in that condition. I can't believe I have to even say that."

He sat down on one of the folding chairs on the porch and studied the watery light.

"Have you eaten?" he asked.

"No. How the hell could I eat when I was that freaked out? Angie was on her way over here when you walked in the door."

She came and sat on the top step although the chair next to him was empty. He said again what he said before, he lost track of time. Harcourt needed to talk. He got divorced just last year, and it was still painfully fresh.

Sam said nothing for a long moment. Then she asked him to tell her everything.

He described the way Harcourt was in college and the way he was now. Quieter, more introspective. He went into detail about his awful family and speculated how nasty they would have been about his failed marriage. Now Harcourt was trying to move forward and looked up an old friend to help him with his venture. And Timothy thought it would be great, to get into home building. It was solid, tangible, and would lead somewhere, not like ringing up customer orders over a sales counter.

"Why did you lose touch after college?" she asked.

"I'm not sure. Just went our separate ways, I guess."

"And then he saw you at work."

"Yes."

"It's sad about his wife."

"For sure."

"Do you think you'll like working with him?"

"We always got along well."

She said she was going to call for a pizza because she was getting hungry. He followed her inside and helped her fold the laundry. Then he rinsed the dishes and put them in the dishwater.

While they waited for the pizza in front of the TV he texted everyone with the same message: *was catching up with an old friend who just went through a divorce. Lost track of time. Everything's cool.*

After dinner, he called Harcourt.

"Dugan," Harcourt answered.

"Good, you didn't crash your car."

Timothy said he was formally accepting his offer and would give notice at his current job in the morning.

"Awesome, man! Glad to have you on board."

They talked for a few more minutes, then hung up.

He thought about the email he'd send to the corporate office announcing his resignation. They'd ask him to recommend a replacement. Jimmy was out. That left Sue and Jiao. Sue had been there longer, but Jiao was a lot sharper. He'd think it over later, then decide.

When the home improvement show she was watching ended, Sam stood up and set up the coffee maker for the morning. She returned to the living room, and stood, looking down at him.

He told her he was sorry again.

"You really scared me," she said.

"Do you think I'd just up and leave?" His tone was light and joking. She looked at him for a long moment then said she was going to bed and hoped he was ready to go, too.

Chapter Six

Sam nudged Timothy awake.

"You'll be late," she said.

"Call in for me. Tell them I got Sue's flu."

She left the room and he heard her on the phone.

When he woke up again it was much later. He got up and put on his bathrobe. Sam wasn't in the house so he checked his phone. She left a text saying she was out shopping and he should have some coffee and take a long hot shower.

He did both. He began to feel human.

While he waited for Sam, he read his other messages.

Lavinia: *I'm glad you're okay. Don't worry Sam like that.*

Angie: *Jesus, you had us all rattled.*

Maggie: *Big Brother, you put the fear of god into us.*

Marta: *Even if your friend was blubbering in his beer you could still have called Sam.*

Sam returned a few minutes later. Timothy helped her carry the groceries in. Potter's truck appeared in the driveway, and Sam said she asked him to come.

"Why?" Timothy asked.

"You know why."

Potter got out, looking fresh and alert. He tapped politely on the back door.

"Hey, Dad! What's up?" Timothy asked.

"I thought we could spend some time together. Sam said you took the day off."

"Yeah. But what about the bar?"

"Matt and Angie have it covered."

"I'm glad Angie's feeling better."

"Yup. Come on, let's take a drive."

Timothy looked at Sam, who was unpacking the grocery bags. She told Potter he could join them later for dinner if he liked. He said he and Lavinia had plans.

"Well, we'll make it another time," she said.

As they were leaving, she looked at Timothy as if she wanted to say something. Then she turned away.

Potter wanted to take his truck. Timothy would have preferred his car but wasn't going to object. He asked where they were going. Potter said just around.

They drove toward campus, then by one of the gorges. They found themselves behind the university horse stables, a set of two large buildings painted red with white trim.

"You know, I met your mother here," Potter said.

"Uh, huh."

Potter turned off the engine. Timothy was glad he parked in the shade because it was another hot day.

Potter said he wasn't one to give advice, but the truth of the matter was Timothy was getting himself into a bad place, and he wasn't going to stand by and not say anything about it. Maybe his words would have no effect—that was really up to Timothy, at the end of the day, but he had to do what he thought was right, and he hoped Timothy ultimately would, too.

"This is about yesterday," Timothy said.

"Yesterday and many days."

"Philosophy doesn't suit you, Dad."

"Don't get smart with me. Your job is to sit still and listen. Can you do that?"

Timothy said nothing. His head hurt, despite the extra sleep.

Potter said people drank too much because they couldn't stand how the world felt when they were sober. It wasn't any more complicated than that. Booze was a symptom of being uneasy in your own skin. Trouble was, that skin was there when the drunk ended and the hangover began. You had to get at the root and figure out why that escape valve was necessary. In his case, it was the way he constantly disappointed Lavinia. He wanted to be the man she needed him to be, and he never could. At the time, he just wasn't strong enough. He had a bad time growing up. His father was a merciless hard-ass who cut him down every damned day of his life. Needless to say, that kind of thing can get to a person, and in ways you don't see right off. He was heartsick all the time—he just didn't know a better word for it—and when he met Lavinia, he wanted her to take care of him. Of course, he didn't put it that way. It wasn't the kind of thing a man likes to say to his bride. He was supposed to take care of her. Then the babies came along so fast, and she was exhausted. Timothy knew the rest—all he had to do was remember his childhood. Jobs were lost after a few months, and the despair, which never left, deepened. It was like looking into a hole every day of his life. So, he drank. Then the hole wasn't so deep and dark. But he failed her, he failed them all, and that was even harder to live with.

"One big downward cycle," Potter said.

"Did Sam ask you to talk to me?"

"She did. And I'm glad she did."

"It's between her and me, you know."

"Not anymore. Not after that stunt you pulled yesterday. She called everyone."

"Well, she shouldn't have."

"What exactly did you want her to do? What would you have done, if she didn't come home and didn't answer her phone?"

"She would never do something like that."

"In that case, you should consider yourself lucky."

Potter said the point he was trying to make was that it wasn't okay to skip out on someone and forget about the time. It didn't matter how badly off this friend of his was. Sam needed to be the most important person in Timothy's life, every day.

Timothy studied the side of the stable. The red paint was meant to be cheerful, but to him, it looked desperate, almost angry.

"Look, you don't know how hard it is sometimes," Timothy said, then wished he hadn't.

"Really? With all that money Chip left you? Living in a house you own outright? He bought it for you, didn't he?"

"Yes."

"And Sam takes damned good care of it and you. Why are you trying to blow everything up?"

"Because I don't want to be taken care of."

"It's her way of showing love. Or is that something else you don't want?"

Timothy opened the door and got out. He started walking, and soon he was out of the shade, in full sun. He left his sunglasses at home. He heard Potter's truck start behind him. Then it pulled alongside him and Potter told him to get his ass in, now.

"No."

Potter parked and got out. He caught up to Timothy in no time. He got in front of him, and when Timothy tried to walk around him, Potter put his hands on his shoulders. Timothy called him an ugly name, and Potter punched him hard enough to send him reeling backward.

"What the hell?" Timothy said, realizing his lip was bleeding.

"If that's how you want to play it, fine. You may be younger than I am, but I'm in good shape, and I'm not hungover."

Timothy just stood there, hearing himself breathe. His lip stung, he was exhausted, and just wanted to go home.

"Come on," Potter said and walked him over to the truck.

As they drove, Potter said Timothy should try to figure out when he started feeling so bad and then what caused it.

"She wants a baby," he said.

"So?"

"What do you mean, 'so?' It's a big deal."

"I'm not saying it's not, but people do it every day and don't go off the rails."

"You did."

"Not until the twins came along. At that point, we had four. I'm sure you could handle one. Hell, Sam would do most of the work anyway, given how she is. And how you are. Not trying to insult you here, son, but you're not exactly a huge help around the house. Even I can see that."

Then Potter said Sam had mentioned something about a new job. Timothy gave him the details.

"Like father, like son. In terms of being a customer liaison. And in other ways, too, but we don't need to hash all that out again," Potter said.

Potter told him to lay off the booze and try to take better care of himself. He said he didn't want any more calls from Sam. Oh, and he and Lavinia were going to have their ceremony a week from Saturday, at their place. And guess what? Patty and Murph would fly out from Helena.

"Yeah? Cool," Timothy said.

"Sam's never met them, has she?"

"No."

"I think they'll get along."

"The twins are coming up?"

"They damned well better. They didn't have a chance to see us get married the first time. None of you did."

Timothy said nothing.

"That was a joke," Potter said.

"I got it."

Potter said he was sorry for belting him, and hoped he understood how frustrated he was—how frustrated everyone was. The one thing about having a drinking problem is you think you're in it all by yourself, but you're not. Everyone else is in it with you. Timothy needed to remember that.

They drove past campus. The sidewalk was full of students there for the summer session. They all looked so young, Timothy thought. It never occurred to him before that Sam might feel awkward, being a decade older than her classmates. She was reluctant even to apply. Her grades from high school weren't great, and neither were her test scores, so she signed up for one of those prep courses and took the tests again. Then she wrote a killer essay about poetry as connective tissue or something like that. He was proud of her, he really was, but her drive always pulled against him, somehow, much as his mother's ambitions must have worn his father down, too, way back when.

Sometimes he felt like he was running a race, trying to keep up with her, though she asked little of him. It was her patience, that air of resigned waiting that got under his skin. But wasn't he the one who was always waiting for his life to change? And now it would. He was ready to work at something, and he never felt that way before, not even in school because grades had come so easily to him. The only thing he ever pitted himself against was Melissa. He took the approach he supposed most men took with women at some point, that she was a thing to be conquered and tamed. Even that was wrong, though. All he wanted was for her to love him, to *know* she loved him, yet he also suspected that kind of knowing, that certainty, was elusive, even with people who had been together for decades.

He didn't need to drink the way he did. He knew that. It was a bad habit, formed years before, something he fell back into when he was under stress, the way another person might overeat or overspend.

Man, his head hurt! The first thing he was going to do when he got home was choke down a couple of Tylenol. Then he was going to suggest to Sam they go and grab that Italian dinner they missed. After that, he'd firm up going to Maine, even though Sam seemed to have lost interest. He'd persuade her again easily enough. He'd have to tell Harcourt he couldn't start until after he came back. He didn't think there would be a problem.

He told Potter about going on vacation.

"Sounds nice. Just the two of you together in a new place for a while. You'll have a chance to talk things out," Potter said.

Timothy wasn't sure what there was to talk out except the baby thing and his drinking. Unless she wanted to pressure him about counseling again. He supposed he could manage a few sessions just to make her happy. It might not be so bad to talk to someone who didn't know him and wouldn't judge him. He could look up Audrey Moss if she were still in practice. She was ancient and that was what, thirteen years ago?

Potter dropped him off and told him to take care.

When Timothy walked in Sam said, "What happened to you?"

"Dad took a swing at me."

"Looks like his aim was good. Why did you fight?"

"We didn't. I wanted to walk home, and he wanted to drive me."

"He wouldn't have you hit for that, but if you don't want to be honest, I'll go back to my work."

She turned away, and he grabbed her arm. He told her to wait a minute. He said his father was trying to get at the bottom of things, and it was uncomfortable, so he sort of clammed up.

"There's more to it than that," she said.

"I called him a bastard."

"No wonder he nailed you."

"Yeah, I had it coming."

She leaned in closer to look at his injury. She suggested he hold a bag of frozen peas on it for a while.

"Okay."

She got him the peas and wrapped the package in a dishtowel so the cold wouldn't burn his lip.

"Why are you so good to me?" he asked.

"I wonder sometimes."

He asked her to sit down with him in the living room. She did.

He said he was thinking about what she said about his trust issues, and he realized she was right, but the person he seemed not to trust was himself. He doubted his willingness to stick with something.

"You've been with me for three years. At your job, what, seven? That should offer some small reassurance, don't you think?" she asked. Her tone was even. He couldn't tell if she were angry and hiding it well, then it struck him again that he lost touch with what was going on inside her. He wasn't the only one who needed to explain things. She needed to do some opening up, herself.

He asked her how long she'd been thinking about having a baby.

An odd light came into her eyes.

"All my life, I guess," she said.

"Even when you were little?"

"Well, no, not then. But when I got older and spent a lot of time thinking about families and how they ought to be, that's when it started."

"So, you want a child to make up for having had a bad childhood."

"In part."

He nodded. He saw himself with a kid, teaching it how to tie its shoes and ride a bicycle, things Potter never did. He was looking at fatherhood through the wrong end of the telescope. Instead of thinking you were doomed to repeat someone else's mistakes, you could see it as a chance to improve on them, and even grow as a person. That's what Sam was trying to say.

"I get it," he said.

They sat for a few more minutes on the couch, each lost in thought.

She said she wanted to work some more on her poem. He asked if she wanted to try the place they were going to go to last night.

"Sure. I'll make another reservation."

"I'll do it."

He took a long nap, and woke up hungry, which was a lucky thing, given how big the servings were at the Italian place. Sam was in a good mood, and he wasn't sure if it were because they talked, or because her poetry was going particularly well. Maybe both.

He stuck to red wine, and only had a couple of glasses. He could see approval in Sam's eyes. She put her hair up and wore a sleeveless green blouse. They discussed his parents and their upcoming wedding. He talked about working for Harcourt. She brought up Angie and Matt and said she hoped Matt was being good to her and not kissing any ex-girlfriends. Every few minutes Timothy thought of mentioning Melissa, but he could never find a way. He was sure the subject would be upsetting to Sam, but later, lying awake after they made love and she had dropped off into a heavy sleep, he knew it was because Sam would encourage him to reach out. She might even say she wanted to meet her. He couldn't get his head around that, even though many people, including good old Audrey Moss, said he had a bad habit of compartmentalizing things. He'd work on that later. For now, Melissa and Sam would have to stay in separate rooms.

Chapter Seven

When Sam realized Potter and Lavinia's wedding was the same day she and Timothy planned to go to Maine, she told Timothy they had to reschedule. Timothy said he was due to start working for Harcourt in just another ten days, so he didn't see how they were going to be able to go at all, in that case. Sam told him to chill, Maine wasn't going anywhere. They could shoot over for a long weekend. She was sure Harcourt wouldn't have a problem with that, right?

Timothy figured Sam was all caught up in the wedding and didn't care about going away. Then he thought she might be disappointed, and was just making the best of it, as she tended to do. Several days of light drinking left him on edge, and he knew himself well enough to know the less he said about anything, the better.

As he suspected would happen, Lavinia drafted Sam and Angie to help her. She wanted white flowers everywhere. She insisted the food be catered, but since time was short, Alma offered to pitch in. She wasn't quite as sturdy as she used to be, but she could still hold her own in the kitchen.

Since he gave notice at work, the mood between him and Sue was tense because he went with his gut and recommended

Jiao for the manager's job. She took the news with her usual flat affect, whereas Sue would have been delighted, which made him feel worse. When she offered to take him out for a farewell drink on his last day, he hesitated. She said Jiao was coming, too. He called Sam and told her the gang wanted to give him a send-off.

"See? You made friends there. You always said otherwise," she said.

"Well, yeah. I think I'll even miss them."

"Go have fun. But don't drink too much."

"I won't."

"We're joining your parents for dinner."

"What? Since when?"

"Since three days ago. I told you."

"Where are we eating?"

"Madeleine's."

"You know I hate French food."

"You'll be fine. Make sure you have enough time to get home and change. That place is fancy-dancy."

"Okay."

They hung up.

He told Jimmy he'd be on his own for a bit. Jimmy looked glum. Sue said everyone had their turn being the low man on the totem pole, and as soon as they hired a new person he'd move up a notch. At the last minute, a crush of customers came in and Jiao said she'd stay behind and help. Timothy told Sue they could go over to Rovers.

"I hate that place," she said.

"Where, then?"

"TGIF."

The bar was in the far corner of the mall. Timothy felt awkward walking beside Sue. He thought he should strike up a conversation but couldn't think of anything charming to say. He was glad there were a lot of people wandering around because it made not talking easier. Sue walked just a little bit ahead of him as if she forgot he were there. When a darting child caused her to stop abruptly, she glanced at him. Her expression was tense, almost nervous, and Timothy wished he hadn't agreed to go with her but figured it would be fine. One drink and he'd be on his way.

Quite a few people were enjoying a late lunch, and Sue went straight to a booth in the back. Timothy asked if she didn't prefer something further away from the kitchen. She said she always sat in the back when she went to a bar. She was used to being a second-class citizen.

"What do you mean?" Timothy asked.

"Never mind. Just my pathetic attempt at humor."

She slid into the booth. He sat across from her. He studied the plastic menu listing beers, wines, and hard liquor labels. He felt like a gin and tonic. It was a perfect summer drink, for a season he despised.

When the server came, Sue ordered a margarita. Timothy said what he wanted, and the server asked if they cared for anything to eat.

"Bring us some nachos," Sue said. Timothy ate back at the store. Sam made him a delicious roasted chicken sandwich. She always made his lunch, though he said plenty of times he could eat somewhere in the mall. Sam correctly thought the food on offer there was lowball and bad for his health. He told Sue she'd be enjoying the nachos on her own.

"You could stand a few more calories on board, frankly. You're awfully thin," she said.

"I'd say I'm just perfect."

She looked at him hard. He looked back. The server brought their drinks and said the nachos would be right out.

Sue lifted her glass and said she wished him well in his future as a home builder.

"Thanks. I'm looking forward to it."

"My husband thinks we should buy a house."

"Now's a good time. My partner says the market's due for an uptick."

They sipped their drinks. Timothy hoped his would make him relax. Then he remembered his dinner date with Sam and his parents.

"And you think it's not?" Sue asked.

"What?"

"Due for an uptick. You looked upset there for a moment."

"Oh, no, I was just thinking about dinner. I'm going out with my girlfriend and my parents."

"Sounds cozy."

"They're getting remarried."

"Who?"

"My parents."

Timothy explained. Sue said she heard of people doing that. It always struck her as strange. How could you know if you fixed the thing that split you up? Wouldn't you feel like an awful fool if you found out you were right back where you started? One thing she knew for sure was if she ever got divorced she wouldn't get back together with her ex for any amount of money.

"Or love?" Timothy asked.

"Nope."

"You don't sound very happy with him."

"I'm not. It's not his fault. We got married too young."

"Not sure why that's a problem."

"In a nutshell, my husband was a kid then and he's a kid now."

Timothy asked what her husband did. She said he worked in a hardware store. He was offered a promotion a couple of weeks before with the corporate office in Binghamton, but he didn't want to take it.

"He says the extra money he'd earn would get eaten up paying for extra gas," Sue said. She took a hearty gulp of her drink.

"Well, unless he got the lousiest raise on offer, that's probably not true."

"It's not. I told him so. He already turned it down."

"I see."

"He's an idiot."

Timothy held up his hand as a request to say nothing more.

"I'm sorry, I guess I just needed to vent," she said.

"It happens."

They drank. Timothy checked his watch. They'd been in there exactly thirteen minutes. He said he was sorry Jiao and Jimmy hadn't been able to join them.

"I'm not. Jimmy's okay, but I can't stand her," Sue said.

"Why?"

"I don't know. She's . . . weird, but not in a good way."

"She does well with the customers."

"I suppose."

Timothy was glad he recommended Jiao for the manager's position. Sue didn't have good insights into people. He'd have to tell Sam about that, then realized it would make him seem as if he were seeking her approval, trying to prove something about himself she had come to doubt.

The nachos arrived and Sue helped herself. A string of cheese settled on her chin and Timothy was uneasy looking at it. After a moment she realized it was there and wiped it off with her hand. He found the gesture crude. Sam would have used a napkin.

"I'm going to miss you," she said.

"Thanks."

"Is that the kind of thing you thank someone for?"

"I just did. So I guess it is."

"You're witty."

"Only sometimes."

"I love you."

Timothy looked at his drink, sitting on the table before him. His hand was around it, but he didn't lift it.

"You don't even know me," he said.

"I've worked with you for five years. I do know you."

"There's nothing to love."

"How can you say that?"

Sue's tone was pleading now, edgy. In a minute she'd break down. He could feel it. This whole time she was been putting on a front, acting as if she were just being friendly with him. The casual flirting of the winter before took on a new dimension. She wasn't looking for a fling, but something deeper.

"Look, Sue, you have to believe me when I say you don't know me. What you think you love—the person you think you love—is something you made up or assumed you knew," he said.

She looked at him with a flash in her eyes.

She said this was what she knew about him: he came from a family with five children; he was the second eldest; the eldest was his sister, Angie, who was a social worker for a long time at the Lindell Retirement Home. Now she works at The Watering Hole, the bar her boyfriend, Matt, bought with a lot of financial help from their father, Potter. Now, Potter had, or may still have a major drinking problem, but so far things seem to be going all right. After Timothy are his twin sisters, Maggie and Marta, who live in New York City on their late stepfather's money. The twins seem to be everyone's sore spot in the family. They work at what they love, but only with limited success, and feel entitled to live as lavishly as they please. Of the two, Maggie sounds more interesting, because she's a painter. Sue, herself, had artistic ambitions once, did Timothy know that? Of course not, because she never mentioned it. Anyway, Marta's probably just as interesting, especially because she's getting a few more acting roles. Her most recent was as the girlfriend of a young man who was in a coma following a terrible car accident. Last in line is Foster, who's about to start vet school. Otherwise, there's his mother, Lavinia, sharp-tongued yet big-hearted, and super generous with her money. Her late husband, Chip, got struck by lightning on a golf course, after which Lavinia sort of lost her marbles and took herself on a solo cross-country trip. And Alma, the live-in-housekeeper can't be overlooked. She worked for Chip during his first marriage and stayed on after his first wife died.

Closer to home, there's Sam, Timothy's girlfriend of three years. Sam had a terrible childhood. Her grandparents were some kind of religious nuts. And that story her mother told her about her father being dead was beyond. Sam's a good poet and wants to make a career in poetry. Sue always wondered how Timothy felt about that, given that he works in retail which isn't quite on the same level as being a poet, or any kind of artist. Of course, now he'll be in real estate—definitely a notch up.

"Did I miss anything?" Sue asked.

Timothy drained his glass.

How the hell did she know all that? He wasn't aware he talked about himself or his family to any extent at all, and here she had details he must have shared in passing. Her brain was a magnet for trivial information. But if she were truly in love with him, then the information wasn't trivial at all, but vital, essential. Unless she were just flat-out crazy. *That* was a definite possibility.

"You're up on the facts for sure. But what makes the inner man tick? You don't know that. No one knows that," Timothy said.

"Not even Sam?"

He took a twenty-dollar bill out of his wallet and left it on the table. He told her to take care.

Sue nodded. Her eyes filled with tears. Then she steadied herself.

"Doesn't come along every day, what I feel for you," she said.

He left the mall by the exit closest to the bar, which meant he had to walk across a wide stretch of the parking lot to his car. His left temple throbbed as he recalled the personal items he forgot to remove from his office at the store—a change of clothes, an old cell phone charger, and a book he was reading the summer before. It was too late to go back for them now.

What did Sue expect him to say? It was her fault her feelings got hurt. There were some things it was better to keep to yourself. Forever.

He called Sam to say he left early and was on his way home. His call went to voice mail. He didn't leave a message, because he'd be home in just a few minutes. When he arrived she wasn't there. Her car and bicycle were in the garage in their usual places. Her phone was on the kitchen counter by the coffee pot.

He went into their bedroom and opened the closet. All of her things were hanging where they always were.

He looked into the backyard and saw her in the far corner, pulling weeds. He called her name and she turned toward him.

"What are you doing home?" she called back.

He crossed over the grass. He explained about leaving early.

She looked at him closely, trying to see how much he had to drink, no doubt. When she seemed satisfied, she kissed him on the cheek and asked if he wanted to go with her and buy a new dress for their dinner out. It was the last thing he felt like doing but he said, "That sounds great!"

Sam was friends with a woman who ran a funky little store over in College Town. It sold second-hand and vintage dresses. Marta worked at the same kind of place in Manhattan for a little while, and Sam admired some of the stuff she got for herself there. On the drive over she went on about wanting something floor-length, which Timothy thought was silly to wear in the heat of summer. He wasn't about to argue with her. She was having a good time, clearly loving his company, and he didn't want to blow it.

The store was small and close and smelled of heat and dust, much the way Harcourt's development did. It was the universal smell of summer, Timothy thought, which led him to wonder if winter had a universal smell, too. It did. Right before it snowed, the air had a scent of silver but were he to describe that to someone, they wouldn't know what he meant. Metals don't have smells. He'd have to explain the air *reminded* him of silver and everything silver is, particularly its color and how it feels when you touch it.

He was still deep in this train of thought as Sam introduced him to her friend, Kayla. Timothy assumed she was some middle-aged hippie with long gray hair and a potbelly, but she was a stunning brunette with high cheekbones. He wanted to ask her if she had Native blood, too, and realized that would be completely off-base. What he asked instead was where she and Sam had met. Both women stared at him.

"We met here, at the store. I told you that," Sam said and moved off to review some dresses hanging along the wall. Kayla went with her. They discussed each piece in turn. Sam chose one and said she would go and try it on. The dressing room consisted of an alcove at the back with a curtain hanging on a metal rod. Timothy could see Sam's shadow as she got undressed.

"Sam says you're going into real estate," Kayla said.

"Yeah. Soon. Next week."

Kayla wasn't as tall as Sam and Timothy looked down at her. Her cleavage was distracting him, and he kept his eyes squarely on hers. She took his gaze as interest because she smiled slyly, then quietly shook her head. He stepped back to put some space between them. Sam was still in the dressing room, humming to herself. Kayla went back to the stool she was perched on when they came in, behind the sales counter next to the register.

"I understand your parents are getting remarried," she said.

"Yeah. Weird, right?"

"Oh, I don't know. People can make mistakes and learn from them."

"And what mistakes have you made?"

Sam appeared in a blue velveteen sleeveless monstrosity that had no shape at all. The color suited her though, he had to admit. He could see her pleasure in it from the way she sashayed, then twirled.

"You look amazing," Timothy said.

"You do," Kayla said. She was flushed. Timothy realized his last question had overstepped by about six miles.

Sam asked Kayla what kind of jewelry would look good with the dress.

"What are you into?" Kayla asked, her color returning to normal.

"I don't know. Silver, I guess. Timothy, what do I like?"

"In terms of what?" he asked.

"Jewelry!"

"Oh, yeah, uh, necklaces. Don't you like necklaces?"

The women turned away and studied a display wall with pieces hung on small gold nails. Timothy strolled over to the dusty picture window and looked out onto the sidewalk and the people passing along it. Their faces revealed little. Some squinted in the sunlight, some were talking on cell phones. A couple went by holding hands and not talking. He loved this neighborhood when he was in college. Whenever he ditched class, which he did a lot in his junior year when things fell apart, he came over here and wandered into the music store that was across the street. His favorite band in those days was Green Day, especially their videos. He was obsessed with music videos in general. Even the country music ones told a story. He toyed with the idea of learning how to make them, but the effort required felt like more than he had in him, then. He worried he had no natural affinity, something he believed anyone had to possess to be good at anything more complicated than a basic task or chore. When he told Sam that, in the context of generally describing that time in his life, she said he might be on to something because, in her opinion, talent was ninety-five percent hard work. She added you didn't know you had affinity until you looked for it, and an urge to pursue something might be construed as exactly that.

A woman walked past the window. For a terrible moment, Timothy was certain it was Melissa, but a closer look showed a forehead that was too wide and a mouth that was too small. She fooled him because she was petite with blonde hair. There were a lot of women like that in Dunston. He couldn't jump out of his skin every time he saw one.

Sam chose a long silver necklace made of balls in various sizes. She was unhappy with the price, and Timothy said it was on him. She deserved it. Timothy passed Kayla his credit card. Sam looked upset. Had he done the wrong thing? Was it some affront to her sense of independence that he buy her a gift? Or was it because she chose it for herself, and therefore wasn't really a gift? His left temple throbbed. He signed the sales receipt and they left the store.

Later, at dinner, the candlelight suited Sam beautifully. Her hair was up, the dress looked better now that she was seated, and the necklace was charming.

"I'm sorry Angie and Matt couldn't join us," Lavinia said. The second glass of wine brought a soft glow to her face. Even so, Timothy saw how she had aged since Chip's death. It was as if she lived through several years in the months immediately afterward. As for Potter, years of hard drinking hadn't taken their toll. For a man in his mid-fifties, he looked sturdy and strong.

"Why didn't they?" Potter asked.

"Angie said something came up," Lavinia said.

Timothy wondered if Angie found out about Matt and that girl from the other night. He didn't know. He didn't want to think about it.

"Someone called in sick down at the bar. They didn't think they could leave. There's a band playing tonight, and the place is going to be packed," Sam said.

"Now I feel bad. I should have stayed," Potter said.

"And miss your engagement dinner?" Sam asked.

The server came to take their dinner order and ask if anyone needed a drink refill. Timothy finished his scotch on the rocks. He asked for a nice glass of red wine, something French, and said he'd appreciate a recommendation because he didn't know anything about French wine. The server was a young woman, probably a college student. She looked flustered and said she'd check with the manager. Potter stuck to his sparkling water. Sam did, too.

Lavinia wondered aloud if they had an engagement dinner the first time around. She honestly couldn't remember.

"Hell, no. Our folks? Give us dinner?" Potter said, helping himself to a hunk of bread.

"Patty did something, I think," Lavinia said.

Potter got a vague, whimsical look.

He said as far as he could recall, Patty held a barbecue at a friend's house. She was still in high school then, he explained to Timothy and Sam, and the friend's parents weren't too happy about having a bunch of teenagers hanging around. But Patty's friend—he couldn't remember her name, and here Lavinia interjected it was Lila—was on board and lobbied her parents like mad. When they learned it was for an engagement, they were pleased as punch.

"Oh, right. You drank too much beer," Lavinia said.

"I tended to do that," Potter said.

"There was some issue with the potato salad."

"I don't remember that."

Lavinia laughed and said Potter knocked the bowl onto the ground and then stepped in it.

Sam chuckled. She had a taste for quiet chaos, Timothy thought. Like when he put liquid dish soap into the dishwasher instead of the granulated stuff they had under the sink, suds flowed out around the closed door of the machine. She thought it was hilarious, even as she dealt with cleaning it up. It was a good trait, being able to laugh at inconvenience.

The talk turned to the wedding. Patty was expected the day after tomorrow, and at that point, Sam, Angie, and she would throw themselves like furies at the decorating project. Potter said he was happy to hide out down at The Hole until it was all over.

The server brought Timothy's wine. She said it was a Burgundy, which meant nothing to Timothy, but he nodded knowingly and thanked her. A moment later their plates came out. The food was excellent, but a little rich for Timothy's taste.

"Who did you find to conduct the ceremony?" Sam asked.

"Judge Rogers. An old friend of Chip's," Lavinia said.

"Awkward," Timothy said.

"Not at all," Lavinia said and looked peeved.

The balance of the dinner passed pleasantly enough.

Sam was quiet in the car on the way home. The sky was bright with stars. Timothy had to admit a summer night could be lovely. He said so to Sam.

She asked why he was so tense at dinner.

"I wasn't tense," he said.

"You sure seemed like it."

"I was fine."

"Why did you make that crack about the judge?"

"I didn't make any crack. I just offered my opinion."

Sam stared out the passenger window as they drove. Then she leaned against it and sighed.

"Oh Timothy, sometimes I wish you could take a really good look at yourself," she said.

He didn't ask what she meant. He was tired and didn't want to have another one of those conversations that circled endlessly and went nowhere. She was under strain from

Lavinia's wedding plans, that was all. Once Patty was there to help, things would be easier.

She fell asleep promptly, but he lay awake watching the night wheel toward dawn. He tried to gauge the time without looking at the clock and couldn't. All he knew was the darkness never lasted long enough.

Chapter Eight

The morning was full of darkening clouds that suggested an afternoon thunderstorm. A cooling breeze nudged the blinds and made them slap against the windows. In the dining room, Sam was writing in her poetry journal. She put her pencil down and got him a cup of coffee. He appreciated the pleasure it gave her to take care of him, though, in truth, he was fine fending for himself, at least where getting his own coffee was concerned.

Afterward, she went to meet Angie at the florist, and Timothy sat with his book about the Incas, which he hoped to finish by lunchtime. Next on his list was a biography of George Washington. What passed as common knowledge of him was a myth and a clichéd one at that. Timothy wanted to know the man's faults, which were no doubt many, given he owned slaves. But then, didn't they all? The better off landowners? It would have felt completely normal, to think of Black skin as property.

He and Sam had seen *Twelve Years A Slave* the summer before. It affected her badly. Timothy tried to jolly her out of it and said it was just a movie about a different time and place, but she wouldn't be placated. She told him as a woman, she, too, was a second-class citizen, albeit not one officially enslaved. He told her she was being ridiculous and she said he had no idea what she was talking about because as a relatively affluent white man, he'd never been discriminated against.

He thought a long time about her words and ultimately saw her point. He never told her so, however, and he should have. Sam wasn't the kind of person who kept score or insisted on being right or needed to know when someone agreed with her. But still, it would have strengthened something between them had he spoken up.

The Incan civilization, ravaged by smallpox and the superior military prowess of the Spanish, essentially ended in 1572. Timothy's civilization would end one day, too. No one would see it coming. It would have been resisting a superior idea or force for some time and then some shift would take place it couldn't recover from.

It was a depressing thought, but then the country he lived in wasn't all that great and could stand to be replaced.

He and Harcourt argued about that one night, back in college. Harcourt said America was the best place ever because people were free to pursue their dreams. Those who didn't get ahead simply didn't want to. Timothy had a different view. Poor people weren't lazy, they just had more than their share of bad luck. Harcourt didn't believe in luck. Every individual started from the same level playing field. When he said that, Timothy got truly angry. He described his awful childhood and said his playing field didn't get level until his mother married a guy with money.

It became clear Harcourt was spouting the garbage he grew up hearing. The guy never could think for himself. It was an important thing to know how to do. Timothy felt he sold himself short by not following through on his dream of becoming a historian. He let Chip's mania about business influence him. Lavinia hadn't cared what Timothy chose to pursue, as long as he stayed out of trouble. That's why he ended up in retail. It was respectable and safe, even though he was overqualified for running a cash register and helping customers find the right size jeans.

His phone rang and he picked it up.

"Hello?" he said.

"Timothy. This is Melissa Cain."

"Hi."

"You don't sound surprised to hear from me."

"Harcourt said you were in town."

"We've been back for a few years. I thought of calling you a million times, but wasn't sure how you'd feel about that."

There was noise in the background on her end. Traffic, he thought. She was outside somewhere. He went to the front window. The street was empty.

"Harcourt must have given you my number," he said.

"No. I got it from the GAP store where you work."

"Harcourt told you I worked there?"

"No. I saw you one day when we were at the mall. That got me thinking it would be okay if I got in touch if that makes any sense."

"Sure."

He wondered which bonehead had given Melissa his number. He bet it was Jimmy. That kid was short in the brain department.

He asked if she were looking for a handout. She said no, Harcourt lent her some money. She was between jobs until a few weeks ago but was working now in the financial aid department at the university, processing loan applications.

"Interesting," Timothy said.

"Not really, but if I decide to go back to school since I'm officially on staff, I get a big break on the tuition."

"Good deal."

They paused.

"I assume Harcourt told you about my son," she said.

"Yeah."

They paused again.

"Is he mine?" Timothy asked.

"Yes."

"How do you know?"

"I didn't have sex with anyone else during that time."

"Oh."

Another pause.

"I suppose you want me to do a DNA test?" he asked.

"Only if you want to. That's not why I called."

"Why, then?"

"I want Mark to know his father."

"Mark."

"Yes."

Timothy said that could be awkward. Melissa said she understood. Something could be arranged, a discreet meeting, if he didn't want his family to know. Timothy said it wasn't his family he worried about, but his girlfriend.

"I see," Melissa said.

"Though she'd be cool with it."

"That makes it easier, then."

He told her he'd have to think about it and get back to her. He hoped she wasn't going to pressure him. She said she wasn't. Nothing good would come of that. Hatred is toxic, she said. She sounded exactly like Sam.

He asked where she was living, and she said she found a nice apartment on West Hill. It was far from work, but close to Mark's school.

"What grade is he in?" Timothy asked.

"Seventh."

He said he'd be in touch. She thanked him and hung up.

He was supposed to meet up with Sam and Angie over at Lavinia's around four. Patty and Murph should be there by then. Foster was collecting them from the airport. That gave him a good couple of hours to kill. Melissa's call had left him restless. He should have agreed to meet her that afternoon and get the damned thing over with.

Would he meet her? He was curious, of course, about this alleged son of his. And about her. He was very curious about her.

He drove down to The Hole. Potter wasn't there, because Lavinia had roped him into her plans at home. The place was quiet, with only a few customers. Timothy took a seat at the bar and Matt came right over.

"Hey, what's up?" Matt said and set down a coaster.

"Nothing. Killing time before I head over to my mother's."

"Ah, yes, the great wedding plans."

"Which require fortification."

"Beer?"

Timothy nodded.

"Coming right up."

The beer arrived. Timothy tasted it.

"Nice," he said.

"New IPA."

Matt checked on the other customers and returned. Timothy asked how things were. Matt said fine, busy. He thought it would rain later.

"Yeah, it's getting dark out there," Timothy said.

Matt's phone rang. He removed it from his shirt pocket, glanced at the screen, and declined the call. He shook his head.

"What's up?" Timothy asked.

"Oh, just that girl, Sharon."

"From the other night?"

"Yeah."

"Why is she calling you?"

"Wants to talk, I guess."

"Only you don't want to talk to her."

"Not now."

What the holy hell? Was Matt getting involved with her again?

He and Matt had been friends for a few years. They met right there, at the bar, long before Matt bought the place. Timothy came in one night alone and they got talking. Then, and other times, they covered a lot of topics, usually about the unfair expectations the world put on people, particularly men. They were pressured to earn money, and yet be true to themselves in the process. It was an unrealistic bind no matter how you looked at it. Matt had his dark moods, to be sure, but he never seemed like someone given to lying and keeping secrets, but how could you tell that about anyone?

"Just don't let things get out of hand. For Angie's sake," Timothy said.

"That's the plan."

Now there was a plan?

The beer went down beautifully and Timothy asked for another. Matt told him to watch it, he didn't want to catch shit when he showed up at Lavinia's.

"And that group can toss it, for sure," Timothy said.

"They're just uptight at the moment. They'll be chill after the wedding."

"You ever think about getting married?"

"Sure, sometimes. I don't know how Angie feels about it."

"Have you asked?"

"Hell, no."

They laughed. A customer took a seat at the end of the bar, an old man holding a small dog. The dog wore an orange sweater. Matt took the man's order, got him his drink, cleared the tables where the other handful of customers had been sitting, and put the tips they left in an envelope.

Timothy relaxed. It was going to be all right, he told himself. He just had to stay on an even keel.

Matt came back.

"What about you and Sam?" he asked.

"What about me and Sam?"

"Do you ever think about getting married?"

Timothy paused. They never talked about it. Is *that* what Sam was looking for? Why hadn't she brought it up, then? She didn't hesitate to slam him about the baby thing, for god's sake. If marriage were important, she would have let him know.

"Not really," he said.

Matt put some dirty glasses into the dishwasher on his side of the bar.

Timothy asked if he had a minute. Matt said sure.

"This has to stay between us," Timothy said.

"Okay."

"For real."

"Okay."

Timothy told him about Melissa. He shared everything, except the part about seducing her on a dare from his fraternity brothers.

Matt looked thoughtful for a long moment.

"Wow, another Dugan out there," he said.

"So she says."

"I think it's cool."

"Yeah?"

"Sure. I mean, you have a kid. Probably. And you didn't have to do all the crap that goes with babies and toddlers and the rest. How old is he, anyway?"

"I don't know. Twelve? Thirteen?"

"That's an independent age. You can teach him how to swing a golf club," Matt said.

"Get out."

"Or anything. You'll find out what he's into, and go from there."

"If I meet him."

"Aren't you going to?"

"I need to talk to Sam, first."

"Oh, right. Yeah, for sure."

Timothy finished his beer alone because a group came in and Matt was busy with their order.

As he drove to his mother's, he watched the sky. It was low and knotted with dark clouds. A sense of hope filled him. He was going to work things out with Sam. She'd be glad about Mark, and proud Timothy wanted to make a place for him in his life. Their lives. She would see it as a sign of his maturity and ability to commit and make things right.

Thunder sounded in the distance. Storms tended to drift down the lake from the north, or up from the southern valley. He couldn't tell where this one was from yet. He was just glad it was on the way.

The wind was up when he stepped out of the car. He hadn't had anything to eat since breakfast and hoped there was something to snack on. He was met with a tray of sandwiches sitting on the kitchen counter Alma was in the process of arranging. She looked tired, Timothy thought. She turned seventy a couple of months ago and was slowing down. Her face lit up when she saw him, and she motioned him over so she could give him a quick hug.

"What's good here?" Timothy asked, meaning the sandwiches.

"Ham and cheese. Your favorite."

She pointed, and Timothy picked up half a sandwich made on rye, just the way he liked it. He asked where everyone was, and Alma said in the living room. Timothy stood, eating rapidly, then he washed his hands and moved on.

He could hear lively conversation as he approached. The double doors to the living room stood open, and Lavinia was at the liquor cart, mixing a drink. Patty turned and saw Timothy and opened her arms to him. Murph approached and shook his hand. He said it was great to see him again. Both Murph and Patty looked like the long-time Montana residents they were. They had pearl buttons and fancy stitching on their shirts, and both wore cowboy boots with jeans. Timothy had never noticed before how much Patty looked like Potter. Same sandy-colored hair, gray eyes, and a perfectly straight nose. Angie looked like them, too. She was standing with Sam over by the windows, chatting away. He went and said hello.

"Hey," he said to them both. Sam hugged him. Then she sniffed. He could tell she smelled beer on his breath. He said he was down at the Hole, killing time.

"Matt behaving himself?" Angie asked.

"Of course."

A loud clap of thunder sounded and everyone stopped talking. When Timothy looked at Lavinia, she was pale. The noise must have reminded her of the day Chip died. The storms that day had been particularly fierce, as he recalled. Potter put his hand on her arm and said he'd take over mixing drinks if she liked. She preferred to do it herself, she said.

Lavinia laid out the plan for the ceremony. It sounded simple enough. Afterward, she and Potter were going to Niagara Falls. She knew it sounded corny, but that's what they wanted, and off they'd go.

Murph said to take pictures. It was a place he always wanted to visit. Then he reminded the group he and Patty hadn't had a honeymoon. They just flew straight back to Montana afterward. Timothy leaned in and explained to Sam they were married here, in the house. Sam said she knew that. It was a nice thing to do, she added, better than in a church.

People mingled. Murph asked Timothy what he was up to these days, and Timothy told him about his new position with Harcourt. Murph was a contractor out in Helena and showed a fair amount of interest. He said he wished he could do more interior trim work back home. His passion was elegant scrollwork, particularly around fireplaces. Timothy said as far as he knew the interiors of the homes he and Harcourt would build would be nice, but nothing fancy, unless the homeowner were willing to pay extra.

"Hell, yeah. Never give it away for free," Murph said and wandered off. Timothy went to find Sam, who was still at the window, only by herself, now. Angie was with Patty and Lavinia, laughing her head off about something.

"Did you accomplish everything?" Timothy asked Sam, as he approached her.

"Finally got her to settle on lilies, carnations, orchids, all white."

"Sounds nice."

"I think color would be better, some pink here and there, but Lavinia knows what she likes."

"She does."

Timothy said he wanted to talk to her in private. She asked if it could wait until they got home, and he said no, not really. They excused themselves and went upstairs to Timothy's former bedroom, which was now a small study no one ever used.

They perched on the wide window seat that looked into the yard. Sam had a glass of sparkling water in her hand, which she set down on the floor.

Timothy told her about Melissa. He watched her face the whole time, trying to see what she felt. She continued to look into the yard. Even her breathing stayed the same. When he finished, she looked at him. And there it was, like a lump of coal just catching fire behind her eyes.

"You lied," she said.

"About what?"

"When we got together, you said you never had a serious relationship."

"No, I didn't."

But that's exactly what he said, he realized. He hadn't wanted to talk about Melissa or the passion he had for her. It would have put him in a bad light, having a woman walk out on him. Now it seemed stupid to worry about how anything looked. Things just were. Sam would have handled what he told her, just the way he handled what she told him about herself. But she had no former lovers, no one serious, at any rate. Her past was drawn by her upbringing and her crazy grandparents. That was hardly the same.

"Sounds like a serious relationship to me," Sam said.

"It didn't last long."

"Doesn't mean it wasn't serious. Was it serious?"

"Yes."

"See?"

"I don't know why I didn't tell you."

"Because you were afraid I'd think less of you. Because you didn't trust me."

"Well, my telling you proves I trust you now."

"No, it doesn't. You told me because there's the matter of this child, and you need me to know because you expect me to facilitate meeting him, and any future involvement you might have with him."

She nailed it. As always.

"I'm trying to do the right thing here," he said.

"Okay."

"Yes, I need you to help me. So, will you?"

"Depends on what you have in mind."

Timothy said they should have them over to the house sometime. Not for dinner, that was too formal. Maybe lunch, or tea, or drinks, whatever. How did that sound?

"Fine."

Sam said she wanted to go home, and she'd walk if that were okay with him. She had to clear her head.

"Let me come with you. I can come back for the car," he said.

"No. I need to be alone."

"I wish I hadn't told you. You're upset."

"No, I'm just thinking about it, that's all. I'm glad you told me."

"Okay."

They sat. He took her hand and squeezed it. She squeezed his back.

"I love you," he said.

"I know."

She stood up and went downstairs. He went on sitting for a few more minutes, then went down, too.

Chapter Nine

Melissa agreed to come over with Mark the following Saturday. She didn't sound surprised by the invitation, excited, or even remotely pleased. Timothy said they'd throw some easy food together and asked what Mark liked to eat.

"Everything," Melissa said.

When Timothy told Sam that, she said to leave it to her.

Timothy had been wondering if he should share the news of the new Dugan with the rest of the family and thought it was better to wait and see.

"Wait and see what?" Sam asked when he explained his thinking.

"If the kid's mine."

"Well, without a DNA test, you'll never know for sure."

"Harcourt says he looks like me."

"Poor kid."

"Get out!"

He was glad her mood was good. He helped her clean the house, which didn't take long because she was always dusting and running the vacuum regularly, several times a week.

Then he hung around the kitchen while she made potato salad and slapped together a few hamburgers. She said she was pretty sure Mark wouldn't like onions on his, but he'd probably go for ketchup and mustard, both of which they had on hand. She went to the store and bought some soft drinks and a bag of chocolate chip cookies. Then she discovered they didn't have any charcoal for the grill. Timothy said he was happy to go for some, but she said no, she should have remembered, and dashed out.

She was nervous, he thought, but then, so was he. He sat on the back porch with his beer, hoping it would calm his nerves.

Thirteen years was a long time. He couldn't even begin to get a grasp on what he was like back then. What he remembered most was nothing ever felt right. He wanted the easy life a fraternity seemed to offer, but there was nothing easy about it. The culture was harsh, and you had to fit it, which meant putting up with other people's excesses. Harcourt said it was a way of grooming the next round of business leaders—you needed to know how to hold your liquor and get along with people you didn't like. That Chip agreed made it worse, but Timothy had gradually come around on Chip by then. He saw it wasn't easy for him to take on Lavinia and the rest of them. A testament to the strength of love, he thought.

Speaking of love . . . He ventured into tricky territory as he probed his feelings for Melissa, or what he could recall of them. Passion, hunger, need. Loneliness, even when they were together; the sense that she was never really there with him, in the same place. He didn't feel that way when he got together with Sam. Passion, sure. Hunger for sex. He wanted to touch her all the time. He still did. But he felt at home with her. Safe. He could rely on her, even if he didn't completely trust her. He was like Angie that way, in terms of trust. Sam was right about that. Their childhood made them wary. But then, Sam's childhood was worse than theirs and she had an open heart. That spoke well of her. So many things spoke well of her.

And there she was, pulling into the driveway. He went to help her. She bought two bunches of pink carnations. He thought they set the wrong tone entirely but told her they were a super nice touch. He set the bag of charcoal down by the grill he took out of the garage earlier.

Timothy had invited them for twelve-thirty. At twelve-twenty-nine, Melissa knocked on the door. Sam answered before Timothy could even stand up from where he was on the couch, trying to read his book on Washington and failing to take in a single word.

Sam shook hands with Melissa, and then with Mark. Mark stood as tall as his mother. Timothy didn't remember Melissa being so short. She barely came up to his shoulder. She hadn't changed. Still blonde, still gorgeous, only . . . she was self-possessed, quiet, almost resigned. Was there sadness in her? There had been before, and he honestly couldn't note it now.

Mark, as Harcourt said, looked like Timothy. It was unnerving, and Timothy refused to let it show.

"This is your father," Melissa said to Mark. Mark hung back, then offered his hand.

"It's an honor," Timothy said. Mark wore a plain black T-shirt and blue jeans. Timothy was also in a T-shirt and jeans.

Melissa wore a dress with a cardigan over it. She had on ankle boots, which struck Timothy as an odd choice for a warm day. Sam was wearing a pair of overalls, no doubt to seem casual, and he wished she put on something nicer. He hated to admit it, but she looked like a hick.

Sam suggested they all head out back. Earlier, Timothy had helped her carry a wooden table from the garage into the shade of their tree. She put the flowers on it. Folding chairs were set apart in a semi-circle. She said she assumed they wouldn't want to sit at the table before the food was ready. What could she get everyone to drink?

"Water's fine," Melissa said.

"Same here," Mark said.

"I've got soda. Or juice," Sam said

"Just water, thanks," Melissa said.

Timothy and Sam went back inside to get the drinks. Timothy took a beer from the refrigerator and expected a look of disapproval from Sam, but she made none. Timothy asked her what she thought of their company.

"We just met," Sam said.

"He looks like me."

"He does."

Melissa and Mark helped themselves to a couple of chairs. They took their glasses of water. Timothy and Sam sat down.

No one spoke.

"Well, Mark, what kinds of things do you like to do?" Sam asked.

"Um, read. Watch movies. Hike."

His black hair was neatly combed except for his cowlick, where some unruly strands make a bush.

"You and Timothy can hike around the waterfall by the lake. I'm sure you've done that before, but it would be fun together, don't you think?" Sam asked Mark. Mark nodded.

Why was she trying to throw them together? Timothy had no intention of taking this boy on and acting like his dad, despite the biological reality of the situation.

"Mark's going to camp next week," Melissa said.

"Oh, where?" Sam asked.

"Colorado. They teach mountaineering."

"That sounds cool."

"It is," Mark said.

What it sounded like was expensive. How could she afford that? Harcourt's money? He said he only gave her a little.

Sam asked Timothy to light the grill. She said she'd go in the kitchen and get everything ready to bring out, and asked Mark if he wanted to come and help her.

"Sure," Mark said and stood up. Melissa had trained him well.

Timothy poured charcoal from the bag into the grill, poured on lighter fluid, and lit a match. He watched the flame rise slowly, then faster and faster. He returned to his chair and picked up his beer from where he set it carefully on the grass. He drank it. Melissa said she appreciated what he was doing.

"I'm not doing anything," he said.

"You're meeting your son."

Melissa sipped her water and looked around the garden Sam had planted. The tiger lilies swayed in the breeze, and the pink blossoms of the rhododendron were shriveled. The bush had been spectacular in early June. It looked tired now, ready for another season to come and go. Timothy studied Melissa's face. He wanted to run his hand down her cheek to see if her skin were still as soft as it had been then. It certainly looked soft. The first time he touched it she was crying. Was that after the confession about getting raped? Or when he confessed he adored her? And why couldn't he remember? It didn't matter. She was here now. Sitting next to him, breathing gently, pushing back strands of hair the breeze had nudged out of place.

"Sam's nice," Melissa said.

"Yes."

"A perfect person for you."

"I think so."

Melissa looked at him then. Some thought occurred to her, something not altogether pleasant, he thought, then decided he was being paranoid and hyper-vigilant.

"I thought you'd be married by now, with kids," Melissa said.

"Why?"

"You were looking for that, back then."

"I didn't want kids then!"

"No, but you wanted a family of your own that wasn't the one you came out of."

That was true.

They never talked about it, of that he was certain. She saw it in him, just the way she must see things in him now.

He asked her how she thought Mark would adjust to knowing him.

"He's known about you all along. I told him he'd meet you one day when he was old enough," she said.

"I see."

She said she wasn't expecting any huge involvement, and Mark wasn't either. It would be an occasional thing, holidays and birthdays unless Timothy wanted something more.

"I don't know. I'm not sure, yet," he said.

"Sam, too."

"Sam, too, what?"

"Sam has to think about it. She's a part of all this."

"Of course."

Through the open door to the kitchen, Sam's voice could be heard as she talked to Mark. Timothy couldn't tell what they were saying.

Timothy asked Melissa to tell him everything, to fill in the past thirteen years.

She sighed and said, "Well."

When she learned she was pregnant, she left school and went home to Buffalo. She told her parents what happened. They wanted her to have an abortion. When she refused, they started pressuring her about adoption. No good could come from raising a child on her own, they said, which meant—and she didn't understand this at the time—they had no intention of helping her. But they were never all that interested in helping her, especially her father, even before she told him about his business partner—which she did after announcing her pregnancy, in the spirit of bringing everything into the open. He couldn't take in the idea a man he respected, admired, and needed financially, got drunk and threw his teenage daughter on the couch in his study during a barbecue when everyone else was outside and forced her to have sex. Her mother didn't believe her either, and she wondered over and over again when she lost credibility with them, assuming she ever had any in the first place. She went to live with an aunt in Ohio until the baby was born. It was all very 1950s when you thought about it. The unwed mother, sent away to a distant family member to cover up the scandal. Mark came along, and Melissa was able to complete her degree at Kent State.

"Yeah? What did you major in?"

"History."

"No kidding."

Not a useful course of study, but it was what she wanted to do. After school, she worked in a bank, then for a lawyer as an assistant. She thought of becoming a paralegal, but it didn't seem worth it. Then she worked for a chiropractor scheduling his appointments. Sooner or later, every boss she had made a dirty joke or worse, put their hands on her. She kept moving on. Then one day she asked herself where she ever felt comfortable, at home, and realized it was here, in Dunston. So, she came back. And here she was. Mark didn't want to leave Ohio because he had a lot of friends there. But he made friends here, which was good.

"What about your parents?" Timothy asked.

"My father's retired. Not chasing dollars all day seems to have softened him."

"Did he ever confront that guy?"

"Later, I think. When he tried to get back in my good graces. In any case, they stopped doing business together. My mother might have suggested it, I don't know. Maybe she had second thoughts and felt it was some kind of remedy." She paused. "They came to see us pretty often in Ohio. I wasn't too keen on that, at first, but it's good for Mark to know them, the way it's good for him to know you."

He reached out and took her hand. He said it was great to see her, he was glad she reached out to him.

"Everything's going to be all right," he said.

"I know it is. I'm good at figuring things out."

He let go of her hand as Sam and Mark came down the back stairs. Sam had a tray of hamburger patties and buns, and Mark had one containing plates and condiments. Timothy got up to check on how the coals were doing, and Sam took his empty chair.

Melissa asked Sam what she did.

"I'm a student at the moment. Also a poet. When school is over, I hope to get a poetry book published."

"That's beautiful."

"Thanks!"

Melissa asked Sam if Timothy read her work, and Sam said no, not really. Poetry didn't seem to be his thing.

"I can see that," Melissa said.

What the hell did that mean? Timothy flipped the burgers and wished they'd stop talking.

But they went on and on. Sam told Melissa more about herself, her childhood in particular, and there they seemed to find common ground, though Melissa had grown up with much more money than Sam had.

Melissa liked the story about Sam going to LA for a while and living downstairs from a little Japanese woman who turned out to be a prostitute. Timothy wondered if that were an appropriate thing to talk about in front of Mark, and when Timothy glanced at him, Mark was texting on his phone. Kids these days were savvy, he thought. He probably knew everything there was to know about men and women except the experience of it.

Did Melissa have a boyfriend? Had there been anyone after him? It wasn't something he could ask, but he wanted to know. What did it matter, anyway? The past was the past. It was the present that mattered.

They ate and enjoyed the cookies Sam put out for dessert. Then they had to go. Timothy told Mark to have fun in Colorado, and not to fall off a mountain. They shook hands. Melissa hugged both Timothy and Sam. Then they were gone. Timothy helped Sam in the kitchen. Afterward, Sam went back outside and sat in the shade. Timothy watched her through the kitchen window. She had her poetry journal, so he thought he better not disturb her. He read for a long time, then looked into the yard again. She was still there, not writing, just sitting.

He joined her. She held out her hand and he took it.

"Thanks for everything you did today," he said.

"It was no trouble."

"He's a nice kid."

"He is."

"Feels strange."

"To learn you're a father?"

"Yeah."

"Life's often that way."

"What way?"

"Strange."

She let go of his hand. The man who lived next door was in his backyard, too, watering his garden.

"Well, I think I'll go back and read some more," Timothy said.

"You're still in love with her."

"No, I'm not."

She said it was obvious, she could tell from the moment Melissa walked through the door. He wasn't aware of it, clearly, and she didn't fault him for not knowing. He hadn't seen her for a long time. There would have been no way to know. But he should know now unless he wanted to dive into another episode of denial, which wouldn't be a good idea. There was too much avoiding truth, and truth was better off faced than avoided.

"Sam, I don't know what you think you saw or didn't see, but I swear to you, I have no feelings for Melissa at all, except mildly friendly ones."

"You were in love with her in college, and now you know she's the mother of your child. If you don't feel love for her, you will soon enough."

"You're the one I love," he said.

She said nothing.

"Don't you believe me?" he asked.

"I believe hearts are complex and can accommodate a lot of love. You can love both of us, in different ways."

"Sam. What do you want me to say?"

"Whatever's true."

"I wish she never came back."

Sam nodded. She said she could easily believe that because life had been one way, and now it was another way, and the future was uncertain.

"What do you mean?" he asked.

"You have yet to see how Mark is going to fit into your life."

"Our life."

She nodded again.

"We'll work it out," he said.

Sam put out a light dinner of ham sandwiches and left-over potato salad. After she cleaned up, she wrote some more while he read. Then she said she was tired. She squeezed his hand when they went to bed. He wanted sex. She turned away, which meant she didn't.

Chapter Ten

Timothy didn't think much about Melissa and Mark in the days that followed. The wedding was coming up fast, and two days after that, he would start working for Harcourt. Sam didn't talk about them either. She was busy making hors d'oeuvres by the dozen even though there were only going to be eleven people at the reception, not including the judge who probably wouldn't stick around.

Variety was key, she said. There would be salmon and cream cheese on crackers, roasted red peppers on crackers, and all sorts of lovely cheeses which had been allowed to come up to room temperature and easy to slice, on crackers. She made batches and batches of deviled eggs, and little cucumber sandwiches with the crusts cut off.

Angie was in and out of the house, offering to help and usually just sitting on one of the counter stools, complaining about everything.

Matt still hadn't called someone to fix the air conditioning in the bar, so she finally took charge. The guy was out the same afternoon and told them they needed a new compressor. Yes, they could afford it, but Matt didn't want to spend the money. He set up fans everywhere, which was a nuisance because they blew the paper napkins Angie set down off the tables. And Potter and been drafted to help Lavinia, exactly what his duties consisted of Angie had no idea, but without him at the bar, she had to deal with all the bills and payroll, too. Matt was no good at those things.

Timothy couldn't stand her yapping, so he went into the spare bedroom, pulled out the chair that sat in front of his computer, and read. Or tried to. He ended up turning on the computer and surfing the internet. He typed in Melissa's name and after wading through several Melissa Cains came to a small paragraph offering the details of a civil lawsuit she brought against her father's former partner. It was dismissed for lack of evidence, but she got the backing of a local #MeToo group that must have paid her legal bills. The lawyer, also a woman, gave a statement to the effect the judge's ruling was another sad case of overlooking a woman's testimony against a wealthy and powerful man.

How did her parents react to the suit? Not badly, if they were in touch. He hoped they were proud of Melissa for sticking up for herself. It wasn't an easy thing to do.

In the kitchen, Angie was exclaiming at the top of her lungs: "No way! No, god damned way!"

Timothy turned off the computer and went out. He asked what she was hollering about.

"You have a son. How long have you known?" Angie asked.

Timothy looked at Sam. He didn't ask her to keep quiet. He just hoped she would. Now he realized of course she wouldn't. She would enlist anyone she could to . . . he didn't know what her thinking was.

Angie had her phone out and was texting away. In the next sixty seconds, everyone would know. Well, he supposed they were going to find out sooner or later.

"What if Mom wants to invite them to the wedding?" Timothy asked.

"She does," Sam said.

"What? How do you know?"

"Because I called her this morning, brought her up to date on everything, and she asked for Melissa's number."

"But, you don't have her number."

"Yes, I do. She gave it to me the day she came over, on her way out."

Timothy wondered whose idea that was.

"Mom didn't say anything to me about it," he said.

"Check your phone."

Sure enough, there was a message from Lavinia. He forced himself to listen to it. She said it might seem odd she invited Melissa at the last minute, but she felt it was the right thing to do under the circumstances. Then she said Melissa sounded pleasant and polite and apologized for not being able to attend the ceremony. It seemed her boy had gone camping, and she didn't feel right coming on her own. She also said she hoped they would meet at some point after her son had more time to adjust to the idea of a new extended family.

"She's not coming," Timothy said after he put away his phone.

"Too bad. I'd like to meet her," Angie said.

"I imagine you'll have a chance before too long," Sam said.

"When the kid gets back, why don't we throw a family shindig?" Angie asked.

"That sounds like fun," Timothy said. He went into the bathroom and looked at himself in the mirror.

You idiot, he thought, examining his reflection. His phone buzzed in his pocket, then buzzed again.

Marta: *I'm an aunt!*

Maggie: *Hey, Dad!*

Foster: *This is unreal!*

Potter: *Wonderful news, but I feel too young to be a grandpa, lol.*

Patty: *Congrats. Can't wait to meet another Dugan.*

Murph: *Say, what?*

Alma: *Is that the same girl you went to pieces over in college?*

Timothy put the phone on the counter by the bathroom sink and tried to take in that his life had changed forever. He wanted to drive around the lake, find a dark quiet bar somewhere, and hide out.

The women were laughing in the kitchen. Angie was saying something about getting a bottle of champagne. How could she go from being crabby to giddy so fast? Sam's moods were much more stable. When she was up, she stayed that way for days. But the same was true when she was down, which wasn't often, thank god.

He rejoined them.

"Congratulations are pouring in from all over," he said and held up his phone.

"We're just one big, happy family," Angie said.

"Yup."

"But seriously, how do you feel about it all?"

Timothy took the stool next to her.

"I don't think I'm used to it, yet," he said.

"It's a lot to absorb. You have to give yourself time."

"Yeah."

"How well did you know this woman, back in the day?"

"Not well. We only went out a couple of times."

"And you never heard from her?"

"No."

"Interesting."

Timothy didn't see what was so interesting about it, but then Angie was no doubt looking at things from Melissa's point of view, or what she assumed was her point of view.

And what *was* that?

She didn't tell Timothy about the baby for a reason. She wanted to be independent, not interfered with. And she had her aunt to help her, she didn't need him. Then it occurred to him she tried to protect him, to spare him the shock of something he might not handle well.

He would have panicked, had he known. Felt trapped. Melissa sensed that and had compassion for him or realized it would have made him an unreliable partner. How could he have been expected to rise to the occasion, at twenty-one? He was a mess in those days, hardly someone you'd turn to with something like that.

The truth was she didn't care for him enough to want him in her life and thinking that again stung. It was time to get over it. He had everything he needed—Sam, a new job, this house, and money in the bank.

Sam and Angie talked about what they were going to wear for the ceremony. Timothy tuned out and sat in the living room with his current read. The book on Washington had turned out to be badly written and dull, so he moved on to one about Julius Caesar. He just read the part where the Senate got him on the Ides of March. Poor bastard. Even if he had it coming, what a way to go.

On her way out Angie patted Timothy on the head and said she couldn't wait to meet her nephew. Then she said she'd see him at their mother's the day after tomorrow.

Two days later, as they were getting ready to drive over, Sue called from the store to tell Timothy about the things he left behind. He said he didn't want them and she could throw them away. Then she said she couldn't find the inventory files on the computer, and he told her where to look. She said she hoped he was doing well, and not to be a stranger.

"I have to go," Timothy said and hung up.

Sam looked at him with raised eyebrows, and he said it was someone from his old job with a couple of questions. She was in a pale pink dress he hadn't seen before with long sleeves and lots of lace everywhere. He would have preferred her in something less fussy but knew she wouldn't appreciate the remark. He wore a pair of pressed chinos and a long-sleeved button-down shirt. The new loafers he just bought—specifically for the occasion—pinched his toes. He planned to slip them off the first chance he got.

Just as Lavinia wanted, the ceremony was simple and quick. It was held in the living room, with the judge standing before the huge stone fireplace that on winter nights had a cheerful fire. As Lavinia and Potter kissed and the judge bestowed his final best wishes, Sam teared up. The twins, who arrived only minutes before things got underway clapped, which Timothy thought was an inappropriate response, but then suddenly everyone was clapping and he did, too.

Then he sat on the sofa and kicked off his shoes. Sam brought him a glass of champagne and a plate of food. He took the glass and said he wasn't really hungry at the moment. She took the plate away. Murph, wearing a bolo tie and another western shirt, sauntered over with a glass of liquor in his hand and sat on the other end of the couch.

"They act like it's the first time around," he said.

"They do."

"When it's actually the third time for each of them."

"That's true."

"You know, Patty and I lived together for a long time before we got hitched."

"Yeah, I know."

Even so, Murph rolled down memory lane.

When they got together there was no talk of marriage, he said. Hell, he would have shut that down pronto, if Timothy knew what he meant. He wasn't going to get roped into anything. They were happy as they were and he saw so many marriages go south, that he wasn't about to throw his hat into that ring. Life was good. Now, he knew he didn't pull his weight in those days, he was sort of experimenting with one thing after another, and Patty wasn't too happy about it. She had a chance to buy the restaurant, and she did, by god. He wanted to bust with pride! And it was getting that deal done that made her want to get another deal done. So she proposed to him. That's right, took the bull by the horns and spoke her piece. He couldn't have been more surprised. Of course, he made the usual argument, that they were already committed as could be, and happy as they were, but there was no talking her out of it. And they've been happy as a couple of clams ever since.

Now, here was the interesting thing, and it took him by surprise. Getting married made you a family, whereas before, you were just a couple. That's why marriage was important. People didn't understand that sometimes. It wasn't just making legal something you already had or putting yourself into a new tax category, it was bigger than that. He hoped Timothy would remember that when the time came.

Matt came over to where they were sitting. Timothy introduced him to Murph.

"So you're the one who landed our Angie," Murph said, offering a hardy handshake.

"The very same," Matt said. He said he couldn't get away before and was sorry he missed the ceremony, but it couldn't be helped.

"No worries. It was over in a flash," Murph said. He stood up and walked over to where Lavinia and Potter were standing with Patty, Angie, and the twins.

Matt plopped himself down where Murph had been sitting. He looked at his phone and shook his head.

"What's up?" Timothy asked.

"Oh, it's just Sharon again."

"Seriously?"

"Yeah. Can't seem to shake her."

"You got a minute?"

"Sure."

"Not here."

Timothy stood up and Matt followed him into the kitchen. They were alone. Timothy asked him what was going on—was he involved with this girl romantically?

"Of course not," Matt said.

"So why are you talking to her?"

"I'm not. She calls me, that's all."

"You should tell her to leave you alone."

"Maybe."

Timothy said he'd try to explain. When Angie and Matt were getting together last winter, Angie said she was upset because he still seemed to be involved with his ex-girlfriend.

Matt held up his hand. "She was never my girlfriend. We worked together at The Hole, and sometimes we hung out."

"Angie says you were having sex."

"Well, yeah."

"You sound casual about it."

"Because it *was* casual."

"Maybe it was, but this girl is after something from you now and unless—pardon my French—you're the greatest stud around, it's either love or money. Which is it?"

"Money."

"What?"

It wasn't complicated, Matt said. The girl was broke and needed a loan.

"But she's working at that bar. How can she be broke?" Timothy asked.

"I don't know, but she is. She's really bad with money."

"And that's a reason to lend her some?"

"Who says I'm lending her some?"

Marta came into the kitchen and said they needed another bottle of champagne. She wore a tight blue strapless dress that instantly drew Matt's eye. Of all the kids, she and Maggie were the "lookers," according to Potter. Timothy came in a close second, at least in Sam's opinion. Marta took the champagne out of the refrigerator and looked at Timothy.

"So," she said. "How does it feel, being a dad?"

"Still getting used to the idea."

"Bet Sam's over the moon."

"She sure is."

She asked him if he could open the bottle for her. She always had trouble with champagne, which was awkward when she invited her director over to her place to celebrate their opening night. He made quick work of it, but then he was good at that kind of thing.

Marta liked to remind everyone how important she was. Timothy smiled politely, took the bottle from her, peeled off the foil, aimed the bottle away, wedged his thumbs under the top of the cork, and got it out fast.

"We could use you down at the bar," Matt said.

"I hear business is booming," Marta said.

"College town bars are a sure thing."

"I never went into The Hole when I lived here."

Marta took the bottle and left.

Timothy was annoyed at Marta's subtle insult, but Matt didn't seem put out in the least.

"Cute," he said.

"Too cute for her own good."

"And the other one is a carbon copy. That blew my mind when I met them at Christmas."

"Yup."

They joined the others in the living room.

Sam was standing at one of the large picture windows by herself. He joined her. She didn't look at him until he put his hand gently on her shoulder. She turned to him and smiled.

"They seem happy," she said, meaning his parents.

"They better be, or they're in for a rude awakening when the honeymoon's over."

"That's a cynical thing to say."

"Why? It's true."

"It may be true, but it's also cynical."

She walked away, over to where Patty was talking to Matt and Murph. Foster wandered over to him with a plate of food he was sampling.

"What's up with Sam?" he asked.

"Hell if I know."

"Come on. She's been moody for weeks, even before you found out about your kid. How's she taking that, by the way?"

"Fine. She's happy about it."

"Good."

Timothy said he'd see him later and moved off to where Maggie was sitting in a chair by herself, looking at her phone. She put it away and said she hoped he was doing okay with what he found out. He said he was doing great and asked how things were with her. She said Manhattan was starting to get to her, and she was thinking about relocating to Dunston and setting up a little art studio for herself. There were a couple of galleries in the city that had taken her on and she could work anywhere.

"You mean abandon Marta?" Timothy asked and finished his glass of champagne.

"I did it before. She'll be fine."

A couple of years ago, the twins got sick of each other and Maggie moved out for a while. Then she went to LA with the guy she was involved with. She returned after a few months and moved back in with Marta.

"She won't like that," Timothy said.

"As I said, I'm sure she'll be just fine. Now get me some champagne, but only if it's French. I can't stand domestic."

Timothy asked Alma, who was making the rounds with a plate of deviled eggs if she'd mind. Alma sighed and handed Timothy the plate she was holding. When she left, he put it on the table by Maggie's chair.

Where was Sam? He found her in the study, sitting on the window seat, looking through a book she took from one of the shelves.

"Hiding out?" he asked.

"I just needed some quiet. I think I overdid it, these last few days."

He suggested they go home.

She nodded and stood up. Angie came in and asked if they'd seen Matt. Timothy said he was with Patty, or so he thought. Angie said he had been, but he went outside for something, and now she couldn't find him.

"Maybe he had to make a call," Timothy said.

"Yeah."

Angie looked glum. Timothy went to the liquor cart, still stocked with Chip's favorite single-malt scotch, and poured himself a large drink. He sipped it. Behind him, Sam and Angie were talking, about what he didn't know or care.

Then Sam was there. She took the drink out of his hand and said, "Try pacing yourself, okay?"

"Sure." He looked at Angie. "What's up?" he asked her.

"I think he's involved with Sharon again. I know she's calling up a lot."

"Jesus."

"Do you know anything about this?"

"No."

Timothy could feel Sam's body tense standing next to him.

"Are you sure?" Angie asked.

"Yes."

"Okay."

Timothy took his drink and left the room. On the side patio, Maggie and Marta were sharing a joint. When he saw them, he held out his hand.

"Tsk, tsk, what will Sam say?" Marta asked.

"Who cares?"

"Ooh, a rebellion is brewing," Maggie said and gave him the joint. He hadn't smoked since college and his throat burned. He chased it away with a large swallow of scotch.

"But seriously, big brother, is all cool with you and your beloved?" Marta asked.

"Right as rain."

"You scared the crap out of her the other day."

"It was just a misunderstanding."

"Uh, huh."

As his mind lifted, he thought of winter, and the color of the sky right before it snowed. Then he considered the different kinds of snow—dry, wet, heavy, light—and the sound it made when you walked in it. As a kid, he got painful welts on his skin from snow finding its way inside his boots, even though they came up to his knee. An image of a steam radiator in one of the houses they lived in years before came to mind, with mittens lined up on it to dry.

He took another hit of the joint and walked off, across the sloping lawn to the road. He set the glass he still held down on the shoulder and walked toward home.

His feet killed him. He stopped, removed his shoes, then his socks, stuffed the socks in his pocket, and carried the shoes in his left hand. Walking barefoot on the sidewalk took him back to his childhood, running around with Angie on the broad slate sidewalks down in the Flats, the neighborhood they lived in then. As he passed through dappled shade cast by a stand of huge elms lining the road, he knew there would be hell to pay for bailing out on the reception. He'd say he didn't feel well and was upset by Angie's questioning and just felt everyone would be better off if he quietly removed himself from their company.

When he got home, Sam was in the kitchen, drinking a glass of white wine. They hadn't had any in the house, so she must have lifted the bottle from his mother's place, or gone to the store on her way.

"I'm sorry I left. I couldn't take Angie's cross-examination about Matt," he said and kissed her on top of her head. She smelled like lavender. He wondered why and then thought it might be her new shampoo.

"I know. It was hard for you to lie like that."

"I had to. It's not my place to rat on him. Especially when he keeps saying everything's cool, and that it's not a big deal."

"Why doesn't he just tell this woman to leave him alone? That he's in a long-term committed relationship?" Sam asked.

"Because he doesn't want to."

"Yeah, but why doesn't he want to?"

Because this girl's attention was flattering, and sometimes a man needed to feel flattered, especially when he lived with someone as pushy and sharp-tongued as Angie.

He didn't say this, however. He wasn't *that* drunk. Instead, he said Matt was trying to be kind, even if the situation called for a firmer touch.

"Well, they're just going to have to work it out, and I hope they do," Sam said.

"Me, too."

She asked how hungry he was, and he said not very. He scarfed some stuff over at his mother's.

"When are they leaving?" he asked.

"Tonight."

"Oh, I didn't get a chance to say goodbye."

"I said it for you."

"Thanks."

He went to change, and she got out her poetry journal and worked away into the evening.

Chapter Eleven

Before signing his partnership contract with Harcourt, Timothy had to show he had fifty thousand dollars to contribute to cash flow if needed. The day before the wedding, he ran the figure by Lavinia, who raised an eyebrow and said she certainly hoped Timothy's former fraternity brother knew what he was doing because she'd hate to see the money Chip worked a lifetime for go to waste. Timothy knew Chip had been born into money, and simply made more, but didn't point that out to Lavinia, because she knew it, too. Timothy drove her out to the construction site and showed her around. She indicated her approval with a brief nod now and then.

The first morning Timothy reported to work, Dunston entered a heat wave. It was already in the mid-eighties and the window air conditioning unit in the trailer was on high. Jack was visiting a supplier up in Syracuse, Harcourt said. He installed a third desk with a new computer next to his for Timothy. The desks were only about a foot apart.

"Cozy," Timothy said as he pulled out the chair and sat down.

"Don't worry, I won't get in your way," Harcourt said. He was drinking coffee out of a paper cup and told Timothy to help himself to one, too, if he wanted. Timothy did. The coffee was terrible. Harcourt wrote down the password for the internet connection and the email address Timothy should use for company business. His first priority was publicity and marketing, and that meant wooing all the local real estate agents.

"You haven't reached out to them, yet?" Timothy asked.

"No. But the model home's finished, and now's the time to get them on board."

"Got it."

Harcourt wanted Timothy to hold an open house and advertise it like mad. Pull out all the stops, champagne, food, the whole thing. Like the old days at Kappa Alpha, only not wild.

"And I'm also putting you in charge of staging," Harcourt said and crumpled his empty cup.

"Staging?"

"The model home's empty at the moment. It needs furniture. Here," he said and handed Timothy a card with the name of a local company that did that kind of work.

Harcourt said there were a few people who were already interested in looking at houses, so the sooner Timothy could arrange for the staging, the better.

"I'm on it," Timothy said.

Harcourt went back to his computer screen. Timothy left the trailer and walked up the hill to take a look at the model home. He should have used the golf cart they rode in the other day, but he forgot to ask for the key and didn't want to go back for it now. The sun blazed, and the air was perfectly still. Insects buzzed in the tall grass just beyond where the dirt road cut through it. Sweat beaded on his forehead. He left his sunglasses in the car. He thought about buying himself a hat with a brim if he were going to spend much time outdoors. A baseball cap would look stupid, but a straw hat with a fancy band would be cool.

The door of the model home was open and he went in. The engineered hardwood floors were protected with plastic. To the left of the front hall was a large room with a fireplace. This must be the living room. Directly across, where an ornate chandelier hung from a boxed beam ceiling, was the dining room. Timothy looked closely at the chandelier and thought it was a needless expense. Why spend money on something like that?

The high-end lighting was repeated throughout. The kitchen had an arched doorway that felt fussy and overdone, but as he walked around the space, it made sense. He had to admit it had a welcoming feel. It was the kind of place where you'd expect things to be good.

Every house his family moved into when he was young brought the same first blush of hope and optimism. There was a tacit sense things would be better, problems would lessen, his father would rise to the occasion and drop drinking, and his mother's hardness, born of exhaustion and disappointment, would soften. It never happened. Over time, there was no more hope, just a practical drive to get settled and hang on as long as possible until they fell behind on the rent. Then Lavinia met Chip and saw a way out. At the time, Timothy blamed her for breaking up the family, then later realized how much his father had been at fault. And now they were back together, everything forgiven. They'd changed. Especially Potter. When he was Timothy's age, he couldn't put his feelings aside, make sacrifices, or compromise. Timothy supposed he was the same way. That's what Sam said, anyway, and she was right. Yet she still loved him. And he loved her, of that he was certain, even if he didn't feel it as . . . intensely as he had for Melissa. They each aroused something different in him. With Melissa, it was the urge to protect and shelter. With Sam, it was . . . what exactly? The desire to receive, to be taken care of, and nurtured. To one he wanted to give; from the other, he wanted to take.

But even that analysis was overly simple. He *needed* Sam. In some way he didn't understand until then, she completed him.

He went back to the trailer and helped himself to a bottle of water from the boxes stacked against the wall.

The staging company was in a strip mall on Route 13, tucked in between a dry cleaner and a pet groomer. A bell attached to the door tinkled idiotically when he entered. The woman behind the desk looked up. He said why he was there.

She pulled out a bunch of three-ring binders that held pictures of furniture, rugs, lamps, framed art, side tables, coffee tables, even bedroom sets, and home office pieces. He said he honestly had no idea how to begin. She asked how high-end he wanted to go.

"Pretty high," Timothy said.

He sat in the chair she gestured to on the other side of the desk.

"Budget?" she asked. She was in her forties, Timothy thought, and not bad looking, though he didn't normally like blondes, probably because there were so many in his own family.

"What does something like this typically run?" he asked.

"How many square feet are we talking about?"

Timothy asked her to give him just a minute. He called Harcourt and ask him how big the model home was. Harcourt told him. Timothy thanked him and hung up.

"Thirty-two hundred," he told her.

"In that case, I'd say around five thousand."

"And how long can we keep the furniture?"

"At least two months. I'll need a five-hundred-dollar deposit to get started."

Timothy got out his credit card.

He asked if it were fairly common for people to stage homes they were selling. She said yes. It gave prospective buyers an idea of how to arrange empty rooms. Some people were good at picturing where things should go, other people needed help.

"Which kind are you?" she asked him.

"Me? Oh, I need all the help I can get."

The woman—Janine—handed him out some paperwork for him to complete. As he filled it in, Timothy asked what style.

"Of furniture? Something modern, I think," Janine said.

"Okay."

"Unless you're really into Louis XVI."

"Which I'm not."

She asked how many houses were going to be built. Timothy said around fifteen or twenty.

"Bet you got a lot of grief from the green spacers," she said.

"I don't think so. That's open country out there. No one was doing anything with it."

Janine talked about the fracking hoopla a couple of years back, but that was a much more destructive process than putting up a house, wasn't it? Local resistance kept the operation from ever getting off the ground. She was proud of that. Upstaters couldn't be pushed around. Let those clowns go wreck someone else's land.

She said she'd be in touch about when furniture would be headed out to the house. Timothy said he'd be there to tell the guys where to put it. She stood up to come around and shake his hand. She was a lot shorter than he was, definitely petite.

"This sounds weird, but would you like to have a drink with me sometime?" she asked.

A charming blush came to her cheeks.

"I'm with someone. In a relationship, I mean," Timothy said.

"The good ones always are."

They shook hands, and he left.

Timothy wondered, as he got into his car and turned on the engine if this would happen if he wore a wedding ring. Sometimes he caught women glancing at his left hand. It would be nice to be able to say he was married, instead of just in a relationship. Of course, he could always lie, as he had with that bicyclist, but he didn't want to lie.

He drove out to the park, sat in his car, and looked at the water. Was he really going to do this? Did he need more time to consider?

"Seize the moment," Chip would have said. Potter would say the same thing. Lavinia would ask him what had taken him so long to make up his mind.

There followed a series of images: the messages that would come from his siblings when they heard; their faces when they came to visit; the toasts they'd make. His newfound son would give him a fist pump because he liked Sam, Timothy could tell. And Melissa? She'd think she missed her chance and look at him with longing when he said how happy he was.

His stars had finally aligned.

La Vake's was the best place in town, something else he learned from Chip, though the man had had terrible taste in jewelry. Timothy remembered one hideous pin he got for Lavinia's birthday in the shape of a bumble bee. She never wore it, though she promised to whenever he mentioned it.

The air conditioning in the store was a blessing, another sign, Timothy knew. A sullen young man stood behind the glass counter, and he perked up when Timothy said he was looking for an engagement ring. He asked for a general price range. Timothy thought for a moment. Then he said somewhere between twenty-five and thirty thousand dollars. The clerk looked stunned.

"Go big or go home, right?" Timothy said.

He was offered an upholstered stool to perch on while the clerk unlocked the case and brought out a tray of sparkly pieces. Timothy confessed he knew nothing about diamonds.

"What is your fiancée like?" the clerk asked.

Timothy said she was serious but down-to-earth. She wrote poetry. She was an amazing cook and loved to garden. In fact, she was an all-around incredible woman. Everyone loved her. Everyone thought she was perfect for him.

"Well, for a perfect woman, one needs a perfect ring," the clerk said.

Most of them were too fancy.

"She's got simple tastes," Timothy said.

In the end, he settled on a two-carat square-cut stone in a wide platinum band. If it didn't fit, sizing was complimentary. Timothy put the velvet box in his pocket and went back to Harcourt's trailer, where Harcourt was in a bad mood because one of the houses hadn't passed its plumbing inspection. Jack had returned from Syracuse. His T-shirt was dusty, and so were his jeans. Harcourt said the failed inspection wasn't a big deal, it would get fixed before the end of the week and Jack said he understood all that, but it had set them back.

"Construction is a study in unforeseen delays," Harcourt said and sipped from a can of soda.

"This should have been foreseen," Jack said.

Timothy sat between them at his desk and told Harcourt the furniture for the model home was all lined up.

"Did you talk to Laurie?" Harcourt asked.

"Someone named Janine."

"What happened to Laurie?"

"I don't know. There wasn't anyone else there."

Then Timothy pulled out the box and showed the ring to Harcourt and Jack. "That's a mighty nice rock you got there," Harcourt said. He asked when the wedding would be.

"She has to say yes, first," Timothy said.

"In the bag, with a ring like that," Jack said.

Jack asked Timothy if he had time to go up the hill and get a crash course on why the plumping hadn't passed inspection.

"Sure. I'd love to."

Once out of the trailer, Jack talked a blue streak. He wanted to be honest—Harcourt tended to cut corners. That wasn't smart where construction was concerned. Inspectors always found out. And they held all the cards. You couldn't tick them off. You had to play ball. In this particular case, Harcourt authorized the use of three-quarter-inch intake lines, when the code called for an inch. At the end of the day, the homeowner would never know. Okay, so maybe they'd wonder why their water pressure was so low, and Harcourt would come up with some story about how the water had to flow uphill, etc. Or he'd blame the contractor, him, Jack, in other words. Jack wasn't going to let that happen. It was a question of reputation.

"So make the decision yourself. Don't run it by Harcourt," Timothy said, hating the heat that made him feel as if he were about to topple over.

"He told me specifically to keep him in the loop."

"Tell him I'm in the loop now and he should just concentrate on playing nice with the zoning board and the good people at the department of land use. I'll suggest he take them out for lots of lunches. Or a few rounds of golf. He'll go for that."

They reached a house under construction and stood in the shade cast by a gracious elm.

"You met Harcourt in college, right?" Jack asked.

"Yeah."

Timothy talked about Kappa Alpha and the wild times they had there.

Jacked nodded and said he never went to college, but his daughter was at the University of Vermont. She didn't seem to know what she wanted to do with herself, and he was all for the idea of taking time to learn and think and all that good stuff, but eventually, you had to realize bills didn't pay themselves. Then he said Timothy and Harcourt probably didn't have much first-hand experience with that, not that it mattered.

"I grew up poor," Timothy said.

Jack nodded again. He said he was glad they had this little talk, and he didn't want Timothy to think he was running down his friend. He wanted to get these houses built and to build them well. That meant no playing games, no messing around, and just sticking to the schedule.

"Why didn't you press the point back there, when he was blowing off your concerns?" Timothy asked.

"You know about his wife, right?"

"Yeah, he told me."

"If you want to know what I think, his old man paid her off. She's Russian. I think she was one of those online brides, or whatever. What I mean is, Harcourt met her online and brought her over. Guess she didn't hit it off with the family too well if you know what I mean."

"You're telling me Harcourt's father offered his wife a bribe to leave him? What kind of person would do that?"

"The father or the wife?"

"Either. Both."

"Point is, he gets super stressed real easy. So, I keep issues to a minimum. I would have dealt with the plumbing inspector, but I was out. Didn't even know he was coming today, but that's how those guys are. Sneaky, you know? Anyway, Harcourt doesn't need more on his plate than he can handle. Which is why I'm glad you're on board."

Timothy had to think for a moment about the fact that Harcourt fed him a line of bull.

"Did they own a flower shop down on the Commons?" Timothy asked.

"Beats me."

Back at the trailer, Harcourt was talking tensely on the phone. When he hung up, he asked Timothy how things looked at the site.

"Good. Just have to change out the intake lines. From now on, let's just follow the code and keep to the schedule. Sound good?"

"Yeah, fine."

Harcourt's phone rang again.

A little later, a couple came by to see the model home. They didn't have an appointment, and Timothy said that was no problem, he was happy to show it to them. When he introduced himself, the husband said, "Dugan?"

"Yes."

"I knew a Marta Dugan. Relation?"

"My sister. She's an actress now. In New York City."

"Wow. That's fantastic. I can see her becoming that. She was always . . . flamboyant."

"She still is."

Timothy grabbed the keys to the golf cart off Harcourt's desk.

The husband, Jerry, was a dentist; his wife, Liz, stayed home with the kids. They were expecting another baby and needed more room. Jerry's practice was taking off. Things were looking up, in other words.

"Sturdy profession, I'd think. People always need their teeth looked at," Timothy said. Liz was heavily pregnant and found getting into the cart awkward. Timothy offered her his hand. He and Jerry sat in the front. As Timothy guided the car up along the path, he apologized for the dust.

Liz asked how long construction would be going on because she wasn't keen on the idea of all that noise. Timothy pointed out that any home they chose would take a few more months to complete and by that time, a lot of homes might be finished. In other words, they might only be looking at a couple of months of inconvenience after they moved in.

As they walked around the model home, Liz wanted to know how much each feature cost. Timothy wasn't up to speed on that yet. He called Harcourt and asked if he could email him a price list. Harcourt sent one, then called and said it was wrong, the prices had gone up, and sent him another.

French doors to the side patio were twelve hundred dollars. Dual sinks in the master bath were fifteen hundred. A cove ceiling in the master bedroom was eighteen hundred. Central air was the big ticket at forty-five hundred.

"Really adds up," Jerry said.

"And keep in mind some of the houses have fewer square feet, so some upgrades just don't apply."

"What if I want hardwood floors in the bedrooms, instead of carpet?" Liz asked. She waddled from room to room. Timothy consulted the price list on his phone and said it would be around twenty-two hundred. Jerry said they had to have carpet. It was cozier.

"Bad for allergies," Liz said.

"No one has allergies," Jerry said. "Besides, you won't want to clean hardwood."

"Didn't you say I could hire cleaners?"

"Yes."

They moved into the walk-in closet. Liz loved it. Jerry thought it was a waste of space, they could do with something half the size. Liz said they couldn't. Jerry asked how many bedrooms the model home had.

"Four, with an option of turning the home office into a fifth."

"I need that home office," Jerry said.

"We'll be fine with four bedrooms," Liz said.

"Not if my mother moves in with us."

"Your mother is never moving in with us."

Jerry looked at Timothy and shook his head.

They asked about landscaping, what came standard, and what they'd have to install themselves. As Timothy talked about hedges and shrubs and flower beds, he realized again that was something Sam could get involved in, at least until school started in the fall. He'd ask her about it. After he proposed.

He should plan a nice dinner, or a romantic drive, or something. Unless he just wanted to walk in the door and give her the ring. Knowing Sam, that was best. He'd take her out afterward. She'd want to wear the ring and show it off, modestly, of course. She wouldn't draw attention to it, but people would see it and make comments. When she called Angie to give her the news, Angie would tell her to take a picture and send it to her, or even better, hustle on over in person.

Jerry and Liz went upstairs, talking about the advantages and disadvantages of having a master bedroom on the first floor. Timothy stood at the bottom of the stairs and waited for them to return. He'd be doing this a lot, he realized, listening to people bicker about a house they would never be happy in. At least at the GAP, the personal lives of his customers were seldom on display.

Timothy drove them back to the trailer and told them he didn't have a business card yet, but he could give Jerry his cell phone number and email address. The husband entered everything into his phone.

When they left, Harcourt asked Timothy if he thought they'd bite.

"I bet they do, and they'll go high-end, too."

"Good job. You want to go have a drink to celebrate?"

"Can't. Gotta get this ring home before it burns a hole in my pocket."

Harcourt looked almost sad for a moment. He said he admired how Timothy had hit the ground running. For a moment, Timothy thought he meant his decision to propose, but then he realized he meant the job. Timothy said he was grateful for the opportunity, and he thought they were going to do something really good for the community. Jack lifted his head from the papers he was reviewing when Timothy said that. Timothy hoped he didn't lay it on too thick.

He was nervous, driving home. He told himself to chill. This was the right thing. It's what they were both ready for.

He turned off the car, smoothed down his hair, and went confidently in the back door to find Angie sitting at their kitchen counter, weeping. Sam was pouring her a glass of iced tea. Sam and Timothy locked eyes, and she gestured for him to follow her. They went into their room, closed the door, and sat on the bed. She said Angie told Matt to move out.

"What? Why?"

"She caught him on the phone with that woman."

"God."

"I know."

They could hear Angie's sobs. Sam said she better get back.

"Wait, I got you something," Timothy said.

"Why?"

"Because . . . never mind. I'll tell you later."

"Okay. Let me get her settled. I told her she could stick around until Matt clears out."

"Should I go talk to him?"

"I don't know. Yeah, that's a good idea."

Sam left the room, and Timothy went on sitting. The ring box in his pocket dug painfully into his thigh, so he removed it, and slid it silently into the drawer in the nightstand.

Chapter Twelve

In all the years Timothy had known Matt, he'd never seen him sober during a crisis. And sure enough, there he was at his kitchen table working away on a bottle of bourbon when Timothy came through the door. Matt looked at him without a word. He'd been crying. Timothy wished he hadn't come over. He didn't want to deal with this right now.

He took the empty chair across from Matt.

"So," Timothy said.

Matt poured himself another two fingers of bourbon, then lifted the bottle toward Timothy. Timothy shook his head.

"She blew the whole thing out of proportion. As usual," Matt said.

"She caught you on the phone with your ex."

"Her name's Sharon."

"I don't care what her name is."

Matt focused for a moment, then got a vague, miserable expression. Timothy waited.

"Why are you still in touch with her? What about Angie?" Timothy asked.

"What about her?"

"You idiot. You made her unhappy, and fairly so. Stop acting stupid. Are you in love with what's-her-name? Is that it?"

Matt said he honestly didn't know. He never expected Sharon to come back into his life. If they hadn't gone up to Syracuse to hear that band, well, that was in the past now.

"I think Sharon should be in the past now, too," Timothy said.

"Easier said than done."

"So answer my question. Are you still in love with her?"

"I was never in love with her. But I feel connected to her."

"And my sister?"

"Angie's great."

Timothy forced himself to breathe deeply. He got up and put the bottle away in a cabinet. When he sat back down, he asked Matt to listen to him for a minute and to focus on what he was saying.

"Okay," Matt said.

Timothy said he wanted Matt to look at things from Angie's point of view. She was right to be upset. She loved Matt. She thought Matt was committed to her and only to her. Then, this Sharon showed up, and instead of drawing a line and saying he was someone else's now, he kept the door open. That wasn't fair to Angie. And to be honest, it wasn't fair to Sharon. In life, sometimes you had to choose. That's just the way it was. You couldn't have your cake and eat it, too. He had to do the right thing and tell Sharon to leave him alone.

Matt nodded. He said he agreed. He knew he had to be blunt. He just hadn't done it, yet.

"It's flattering when a woman shows an interest in you. And it can be hard to say no. But the consequences of not saying no are way worse than the fun of saying yes," Timothy said.

Matt sighed. He looked at his empty glass and noticed the bottle was gone. If he moved to get it, Timothy wouldn't let him.

"I guess that chick, Melissa, hasn't made her move yet," Matt said.

"What are you talking about?"

"The mother of your child, dummy."

"Speak plainly."

"It's easy for you to talk about making smart choices, but when Melissa tells you you're the love of her life, you won't find it so easy to do the right thing. Or even to figure out what the right thing is. Hell, she'll have your kid on her side. What will Sam have?"

Timothy looked out the window. The earlier clouds had cleared, and the sky was ablaze with light. A jet trail cut across, thin at one end, gradually widening and growing soft at the other. The people on that plane might look down on the rolling country around Dunston, comment on the size of the lake, and how charming it all was. Maybe they lived somewhere flat and longed for a more interesting landscape.

"I'm not the love of her life, and never was," Timothy said.

"But, is she the love of yours?"

"Listen, Matt, Angie's over at my place, crying her eyes out because of you. So, here's what you're going to do. You're going to sober up, take a shower, and go over and bring her home. You're going to tell Sharon enough is enough."

"I'll send her a text."

"No time like the present."

Matt dug his phone out of his pocket and stared at it. Then he typed something in. He passed the phone over to Timothy.

Sharon, you have to stop calling me. I'm involved with someone else. Leave it where it all is.

The message listed her as the recipient.

Timothy told him to call Angie now and tell her what he did.

"And do something really, really nice for her afterward. Take her to dinner. Buy her something she's had her eye on. Shower her with love and affection, or I swear, I will come back here and kick your ass."

Timothy said he'd give him some privacy and went into the living room. He heard Matt on the phone. Angie did most of the talking. Then Matt said, "I know. I'm sorry. Sit tight, I'll be there soon."

Timothy told him to go take a shower, and then he'd drive him over. Angie would bring him back.

Matt had a glass of water and went into the bathroom. Timothy got the bottle and poured himself some bourbon into a coffee cup he rinsed out from the sink. He drank it quickly. On the table behind him, Matt's phone buzzed. Timothy picked it up.

Are you kidding me right now? What about all that stuff you told me last night?

Timothy typed. *I was drunk. Leave me alone.*

There was a pause, and then Sharon wrote back *JERK.*

Timothy put the phone back where it had been. He thought about having a second drink. That wouldn't be a good idea at the moment, even though the whole situation with Matt and Sharon had left him as tight as a drum. He was angrier than he realized. You just didn't do that kind of thing, not if you were a decent person. If things were different, Timothy might just urge Angie to break it off. But she was in it up to her ears now, since Potter owned most of the bar, and she quit Lindell to work there, too. Then again, it was her problem, not his. She had her doubts about Matt, and went ahead, anyway.

After what felt like a long time, Matt returned. His hair was wet and neatly combed. They didn't talk on the way over, then as they pulled into the driveway, Timothy said, "Sorry to have strong-armed you back there."

"It's okay. I deserved it."

They went in. Sam was washing dishes. Angie sat at the counter where she was before. She looked at them both with stormy eyes. Matt told her they were going home, everything was fine, he wasn't going to talk to Sharon anymore, and if he ever went back on that, she could help Timothy kick his ass.

"Oh, I'll do it on my own, thanks," Angie said, but she didn't sound mad. She looked worn out. She thanked Sam for letting her come over and said she wished the circumstances had been cheerier. Matt looked like he might want to hang out for a while, and Timothy was glad when Angie stood up and said they were leaving.

Sam told Angie to call her later if she wanted.

When they left, Sam dropped down into a chair at the dining room table and said, "Man, that guy. I don't know how she stands it."

"Me either."

"How did you get him to agree to leave that woman alone?"

"I threatened him."

"Get out."

"Okay, I impressed upon him the necessity of doing the right thing."

"I would love to have been there."

What did she mean? He was exaggerating? Or outright lying? Maybe she just meant she would have liked to see Matt get what was coming to him.

She said she better go start thinking about dinner.

"Hold on," said.

"What?"

"Now that my dear sister has returned to romantic bliss, I have something for you."

"Oh, right. I forgot."

Timothy went and got the ring box. He came in with it behind his back. He told Sam to close her eyes, and when she had, he set the box on the table in front of her. He told her to open her eyes. She did. She saw the box immediately. Her face had been bright with anticipation before. It stilled. Her eyes were dark. Then she sighed. She reached for the box, picked it up, and didn't open it.

"Go on," he said. He was sitting now, too.

She lifted the lid, took a long look at the ring, and put the box on the table.

"Timothy," she said.

"Don't you like it?"

"It's gorgeous. And it's all wrong. All wrong for me, that is."

"What are you talking about?"

She put both her hands on the table and asked him to look at them. He did. She told him to note they weren't small or delicate, but big, and sturdy. Not what you'd think of as the hands of a poet, but she hadn't always been a poet, had she? She cleaned motel rooms with these same hands, and before that, defended herself against her vicious grandmother, and punched a couple of kids before that who were picking on someone they shouldn't have. These hands pulled weeds and scrubbed out cabinets. They were good, capable hands, and she was proud of them. She wanted him to tell her when she ever wore a ring, any kind of ring, in the time they'd been together.

"I guess you haven't," he said.

"I'm not much for jewelry, except for a necklace, now and then. I do like the one you just bought for me, by the way. Thank you again for that."

She leaned in and kissed his cheek.

"But, this is an engagement ring," he said.

"I know."

That was another thing, she said. When they first got serious, right around the time they thought about moving in together, they talked about marriage. Did he remember? She said she wasn't interested in it. That the whole idea sat badly with her. Then, as now, her feeling was no doubt influenced by the nonsense her mother told her about her father when she was little. Anyway, that was history. Ancient history. The point was, it made her think about marriage as this kind of trophy, a prize awarded for devotion. It was a fine idea for some people, just not for her.

"But you want to have a baby," Timothy said.

"So? You don't have to be married to do that. Lots of people have children without being married these days. There's nothing wrong with it."

"I thought this was what you wanted."

"I *never* said it was, and that's the problem."

She pushed the ring box toward him. She looked tired from having had to deal with Angie, he thought. She took his hand and asked him when he stopped seeing her, and stopped knowing the person she was.

"Sam," he said.

"I've been here the whole time, you know."

They sat, still holding hands across the table. His left temple throbbed. Everything she said was true. She wasn't interested in rings, or in getting married. What the hell was he thinking?

Melissa's shadow took on substance within him. The ring he bought was something she'd go for. She had patrician tastes. He recalled the small, elegant diamond earrings she wore to the barbecue and the slim gold bracelet on one wrist. He tried to picture her hands but couldn't. All he remembered of them was they were clean and soft. Had they been on his mind when he bought the ring?

"Christ," he said.

"It's okay. I'm glad we were able to talk about this."

"Yeah."

"Can you get the money back?"

"For the ring? I can try."

She sat for a moment, then released his hand. She said if he wanted to do something for her, he would follow through on counseling.

He nodded.

"How was your first day with Harcourt? I completely forgot to ask you about that."

He told her everything. She said Harcourt's story about his wife was wild and asked if Timothy had second thoughts now, putting his money on the line with someone who had trouble being honest. He said it was all right, the business was solid, and he thought they'd see a good profit come spring. Frankly, all he cared about was the bottom line.

Sam said she wondered how his parents were enjoying Niagara Falls. Then she reminded him Patty and Murph were still in town for a couple of more days, and it might be nice to see them before they left. Patty had mentioned wanting to go check out The Hole, sort of to compare it to the place she owned out in Helena. When she said this, his eyes lifted.

"That's a great idea," he said.

"Taking Patty to The Hole?"

"Yeah. Let's do that."

Sam nodded. He could see something else was on her mind.

She asked if he'd been thinking about Mark. He said he had. She suggested he might send him a text just to say hi and see how he was liking Colorado. He could get the number from Melissa. Sam was sure she wouldn't mind his having it.

She let go of his hand and opened the ring box. She removed the ring and slid it on her finger. She struggled to push it past the knuckle and extended her hand to regard it from a greater distance.

"It's gorgeous, I have to admit," she said.

"Wear it for a while. It might grow on you."

"I don't imagine it would hinder my poetry any, do you?"

"Is that what you're worried about, seriously?"

"I don't know. I'm afraid of getting too comfortable."

"In that case, think about how disruptive having a baby would be."

"Oh, I have."

She turned her hand this way and that, letting the stone catch the light.

Then she took it off and put it away. When she saw his expression, she said if she wore it, people would assume something they hadn't yet decided on.

"So, it's not out of the question?" he asked.

"Nothing is out of the question. I didn't mean to imply that."

"Just you're not an engagement ring kind of person."

She looked at the ring again, sitting in the open box.

"Well, I have a feeling that might just change," she said. But she left the ring where it was. She asked what he wanted for dinner. He said he was in the mood for fried chicken, and she said she'd get on it.

As they ate, she said she wished they'd spent more time with Mark and hoped they'd see a lot of him when he got back. Timothy said he'd be busy with school. Sam wondered what subjects he was good at, and which he dreaded. Timothy said if he were anything like his old man, he'd love history and hate math.

The next evening, Timothy and Sam took Patty and Murph down to The Hole. Patty mentioned several ways the bar could be improved, putting the lack of air conditioning at the top of her list. Angie sat with them for a bit after serving their drinks. Neither Patty nor Murph knew about the recent issue with Matt, and Timothy hoped Sam wouldn't bring it up. She didn't. Instead, she asked Patty about Montana. Patty was in love with the place; Murph was, too, but then, he grew up out there and never left to go anywhere except to visit.

Angie went back to work. The conversation at the table was light and pleasant, and they ordered a second round. Now and then Timothy glanced over at Matt to see if he were on his phone, and he never was. His expression was calm and easy, and Timothy wished he knew what he was thinking.

Murph asked when Mark was coming back from camp. Sam said in a couple of weeks.

"What's it like to suddenly find out you're a dad?" Patty asked.

"Weird."

"Man, I bet. Hard to imagine," Murph said.

"You'll find out when one of your ex-girlfriends shows up with Murph Jr.," Patty said in a teasing voice. Murph said that given how long they'd been together, the kid, person, child, would be at least twenty and not looking for a dad at that point.

Sam told them about discovering her father a couple of years ago. She got used to the idea she'd never know who he was, and when she found out, she was glad. They were in touch a couple of times a year.

"Have you met him?" Patty asked Timothy.

"No."

"Don't you want to?"

"That's up to her."

Sam said she wanted to take things slow.

The conversation moved on to how hot it got in Montana in July and August, and how there was always a forest fire somewhere. Murph held up his hand to signal he wanted another round, and Patty pulled it back down. She told him flying was no good with a hangover. Murph said that was the best time to fly and put his hand up again.

Timothy dropped into himself. Why didn't Sam want him to meet her father? What was she waiting for, to see if they'd last as a couple? It had never bothered him before, but the guy didn't live far away, just a few blocks over, so what was the deal? He was a therapist. Timothy could see him professionally, but that wouldn't work, would it? Like a surgeon who won't operate on a family member. Of course, that assumed Sam would come up as a subject. Well, she'd have to, wouldn't she?

His phone buzzed in his pocket and he pulled it out. It was Melissa. He declined the call. When Sam and Patty got up to visit the Ladies' room, he listened to the message.

"Hi, I'm sorry to bother you, but something's been on my mind I should have brought up at the barbecue and just didn't know how. The thing is, I've been having trouble with Mark. He's a good kid, but he's growing up fast and needs a male role model. I'm not involved with anyone at the moment, and won't be for a long time, and wouldn't want to count on that person for that in any case. Long story short, how would you feel about a shared custody arrangement? Sorry to spring this on you, but I've been thinking about it for a while. And Mark suggested it himself after he met you. Talk to Sam, and see what you think. I wouldn't expect you to pick up his expenses. I'll cover those. Okay, that's it, bye."

Timothy put his phone away. Murph said he looked like the bottom just fell out of the housing market. In any case, he hoped it wasn't bad news.

"Everything's cool. What about that round?" Timothy asked.

Later, after lots of hugs and handshakes and promises to come to see them in Montana, Sam and Timothy went home and turned in early.

The next day, the furniture arrived for the model home. The delivery guys took charge of where it should go. Timothy asked them to adjust the sofa in the living room so that it faced the fireplace. When they were done, he walked around the place and thought it looked great. Harcourt wandered up from the trailer and strolled around, too. He said he didn't like the rug they put in the dining room, but it didn't matter. He said he was thinking of raising the price of the home by at least ten grand, based on a conversation he had with a realtor over dinner the night before.

"Have you checked what things are selling for?" Timothy asked.

"Frank did that. The realtor. He says we're coming in low."

Harcourt was dressed in a pair of shorts and a T-shirt, as was Timothy, against the heat. Timothy wished they could turn on the air conditioning in the model home. Harcourt said it was all hooked up and ready to go, but he didn't want to run up a big bill before the place had even sold.

They went to view a house under construction and talked to one of the workers there, who said they were waiting on a couple of deliveries, one for siding, and the other for roofing. They walked on the plywood floors. It was odd to see the entire layout through the studs waiting for drywall to go on. The sound of a staple gun made it hard to talk, and they went outside, where a future patio was staked off. Harcourt said he could see a couple of chairs and a grill, maybe a planter.

At the next site, a foundation had been poured, and part of it was in shade. Harcourt sat on one of the concrete blocks and looked at his phone. Timothy joined him. The view of the lake was lovely, and he hoped the house would be oriented to take full advantage of it. What would the people be like who lived there? Happy? In love? At peace with the choices they made?

Sam would push him to accept Melissa's offer of shared custody. She'd say it was a trial run, a chance to develop his fathering skills. It wasn't a bad idea. He could see himself helping Mark with his homework, driving him to school, and making his lunch. He wasn't sure how he felt about having Melissa that much more in his orbit. He was still mad for her on some level and didn't want that feeling to run away with him. Then again, spending more time together might cool him down, and give her a chance to reveal some annoying trait that made him glad it didn't work out between them.

"Look, Jack may have said some things about me that might have sounded weird," Harcourt said.

"Like what?"

"Oh, I don't know. Random stuff."

"He didn't say anything. We just talked about the project."

"Cool. That's what he's here for."

"Me, too."

Harcourt asked when Timothy thought the open house might be held at the model home.

"How about a week from Saturday? I'll get Sam to help me."

"That would be awesome. I have to meet this amazing lady of yours."

"She'd like to meet you, too."

"Good deal."

They went back to the trailer, which was theirs for the moment since Jack was out. Harcourt said he was scheduled to take a couple of realtors to lunch. Did Timothy want to join? Timothy said he needed to get to work on the open house, but Harcourt should be sure to invite the realtors to that. He asked if he had any ideas for a flyer they could use to advertise it.

"I've got a mock-up on my computer. I'll send you the file," Harcourt.

"Cool, thanks."

The graphic was too plain, so Timothy put it on a thumb drive and drove over to a local copy center. He told the guy at the counter what he was looking for was a green background and white lettering, something summery. The clerk suggested a stock photo of Lake Dunston since the development was called Lakeland Estates. Timothy wasn't sure, and the guy said he'd mess with it for a while, and email over some options.

Next, he stopped by the catering company his mother used for the wedding. It was part of a small specialty food store that sold high-end olive oil, cookware, wine, sandwiches, and baked goods. He mentioned Lavinia's name to the woman there, and she said she remembered her.

"I'm Adele," she said and shook his hand.

"Timothy."

He asked what would be good for a real estate open house. She said finger food, small bites, stuff people could eat easily. They had a standard menu for that kind of thing—they catered a lot of faculty events on campus. Academics went for the high-end items, like smoked salmon and imported cheese, probably because their salaries were so meager. Her husband taught in the French department and was always disappointed by his raises, though she shouldn't say so. Timothy gently cut her off and asked if he could trust her to put a menu together and let him know later how much it would cost. She seemed delighted at the idea. He asked her to email him the details when she had them.

He called Sam when he got in the car.

"Hello?" She sounded rushed.

"Hey. I forgot to mention, I'm putting together this open house a week from Saturday and I want to know if you can come."

"I don't see why not. Wait, no. Oh, never mind. That's the Saturday after."

"What is?"

"The poetry reading."

"I thought that was last month."

"It was. This is a different one. Professor Wells just emailed me about it."

"Who?"

"Steven Wells. My professor."

"Okay."

He never heard of him, but that didn't matter. She said she was in the middle of a poem, a good one, or so she thought, and could they talk later, when he got home?

"Sure. Love you," he said.

"Love you, too."

They hung up. Timothy watched the traffic on the highway and thought about going to Maine. He wished they'd gone. He wanted to get out of town for a while.

He was almost desperate to.

Chapter Thirteen

Harcourt fell behind on the utility bills for the development, and the electric company shut off its power two days before the open house. They wouldn't accept payment over the phone, so he went down to the office and paid in cash, just to fluster the clerk. The bill was close to a thousand dollars. Harcourt paid in fives and tens, and it took the clerk, some old lady with a nasty mole on her cheek, three tries to count the sum correctly. Timothy thought Harcourt's time would have been better spent paying the bill when it came in, rather than turning it all into some big joke.

Everything now had power, and the construction crew was back at work, but the air conditioning at the model home wouldn't turn on, and the service technician was an hour late. Timothy had been on the phone twice trying to nail down his arrival time with no luck. Finally, he showed up, took a look at the compressor, and said the control board was bad. He didn't have a replacement with him, so he'd go back to town and get it. He'd try not to be too long. When he left, Timothy told Harcourt the vendor would have to reimburse them for the service call.

"What do you mean?" Harcourt asked.

"The compressor's under warranty, right?"

"No."

"Didn't you buy it new?"

"Second-hand."

Timothy swiveled his chair toward Harcourt and said, "Stop cutting corners. That's what got you into trouble with the plumbing inspector."

"I wasn't cutting corners. I was trying to save us money."

"Well, that's not the way to do it."

"Since when did you become such an expert?"

"Since I sweat bullets putting together an open house that's going to be held without air conditioning. It's ninety degrees out, or haven't you noticed?"

Harcourt said the air conditioning would get fixed, the open house would be great, and he didn't appreciate being told how to run his business. He hoped Timothy would keep that in mind next time.

"Your business? I thought this was our business," Timothy said. The blinds on the trailer windows were down but daggers of light cut through.

"Man, I forgot how pushy you can be. I should have remembered that before I took you on."

"Look, if you think you made a mistake, I'll be on my way. Trust me, I don't need this grief." Timothy stood up and Harcourt raised his hand.

"Chill out, you're right. No good cutting corners."

Timothy went on standing. His left temple throbbed. Harcourt looked at something on his computer and wouldn't meet his eye. Same old Harcourt, he thought. Starts a fight, then walks away before it's over.

The service technician returned. Timothy was still keyed up from his tiff with Harcourt, so he walked with him up the hill to the broken compressor. The guy asked if he were related to a Foster Dugan.

"My little brother," Timothy said.

"Is he still into animals?"

"Studying to become a vet."

"No kidding. That's awesome."

The technician—Bruce—took the top off the compressor and said it wouldn't take him long to replace the control board. Should he leave the bill, or ask the office to send it?

"Have them send it. I need to get back."

"Sure. No problem."

When he returned to the trailer, Jack was there, studying a set of plans with Harcourt. A young woman sat sullenly on the couch, looking at her phone. Timothy introduced himself.

She said she was Sasha, Jack's daughter.

"Right. You're at UVM," Timothy said.

"Uh, huh."

Sasha had black hair and olive skin and didn't look anything like Jack. Maybe she was adopted. Maybe her mother was Middle Eastern. Jack didn't seem like the kind to go for an exotic type like that, but who knew? Timothy asked if he could get Sasha a cup of coffee. She stared at him, then said she was fine.

"Water?" Timothy asked.

"Sure."

He got her a bottle from the stack of boxes along the wall and gave it to her. She put it on the floor and went back to studying her phone.

Timothy sat at his desk and reviewed his emails. One was an update from the caterer. Along with sparkling water, and a variety of soft drinks, she suggested a nice California chardonnay, which was perfect for summer. She also said the young man who usually did the serving at these events was on vacation and she'd have to come herself. She hoped Timothy didn't mind. He replied that it wasn't an issue at all, chardonnay was great, and asked her to bring along a couple of bottles of champagne. He reminded her to tell everyone she knew about the event, and say they were welcome to come, too.

The rest were from people who wanted to tour houses. He pulled up the appointments spreadsheet and began entering names then realized he should call first, in case there was a scheduling conflict. When he got out his cell to dial the first number, Jack and Harcourt's conversation turned loud. They weren't arguing, exactly, just being emphatic. Jack had a guy in mind to do stonework, and Harcourt said his guy was cheaper.

"It's not going to happen, Jack," Harcourt said.

"Calm down. Let's call him up, and see what he has to say."

Sasha looked at her father. "I need to get going," she said.

"Just a few more minutes, hon. Then I'll drive you," Jack said.

Sasha caught Timothy's eye. He asked her where she had to go. She said home, over in Lansing. It wasn't far.

"I'll take you. I've got some errands to run, anyway," he said.

"Won't it be out of your way?"

"On a beautiful summer day like this, driving's a pleasure. Especially with such a charming passenger."

Sasha tried to get Jack's attention. When she failed to, she stood up and walked out of the trailer. Timothy followed. He pointed out his car.

"Nice," she said and got in.

"It's a money pit."

"Like those houses of yours."

"Come again?"

As they drove she explained. He shouldn't say where he heard this from, but Jack got sued by a property developer a few years ago for shoddy construction. Part of a roof gave way and a child was hurt. In the court case that followed it couldn't be proven Jack had known or approved of the substandard building materials used, but he almost lost his license and had had a hard time getting the state to reissue his bond. That's why he was focused on doing everything by the book.

Timothy wondered if Harcourt knew all that, or if he hired Jack specifically to do things on the cheap, figuring he did once or might have at any rate. He didn't share that with Sasha. He just said Jack seemed like a really solid guy and from everything he'd seen so far, the work was first-rate.

"You're a born salesman," Sasha said. She played with the radio. An oldies station came up. Timothy didn't like listening to music when he drove. He adjusted the air conditioning so it blew on his face.

Sasha asked how long Timothy had been working for Harcourt. Timothy told her. Then she asked if he were from around there.

"Born and raised," he said.

"Poor you."

"You don't like Dunston?"

"It's all right. I'm just not going to die here."

"You have a lot of time between now and then."

"Not if you don't slow down."

Sam told him he drove too fast when he was nervous and she was right. Why was he nervous now?

Because Sasha was giving him the eye.

She told him which road to take. He followed her directions, and after a few more minutes, they came to an empty field in the middle of nowhere. He asked her what the hell she thought she was doing.

"This," she said, and leaned over to kiss him on the mouth. He kissed her back. She tasted like mint and smelled like cinnamon.

He pulled away.

"You're not going to stop there, are you?" she asked. He felt the warmth of her breath on his face. He wanted to pull her out of the car, tumble into the shade, and make love to her so hard she sank into the earth.

"Yes," he said.

Sasha pulled back into the space of her seat. Blood thudded in his ears, and his vision narrowed for a moment, then returned to normal. He rolled down his window. The air that came in was warm and smelled of cut grass. Sasha looked straight ahead. She seemed bored as if she were waiting for a traffic light to change.

"Okay. Whatever you say," she said.

She gave him the correct directions this time, and they arrived at a renovated farmhouse shaded by a gorgeous old elm tree. The wraparound porch was deep. It looked like a lovely place to sit and think. Sam would like it a lot. It was the sort of home he could see her in.

He didn't want to think about Sam now. The guilt over kissing Sasha was rising fast. He glanced at her again. She still looked bored. She thanked him for the ride and got out of the car.

Timothy headed for home. Sam was out. She texted to say his parents were back and she was over there visiting. Dinner was at six. He should come a little early if he could.

He got himself a drink in the kitchen. Then he had another one. After that, he went into the spare room and turned on the computer. He logged in to his work email account and called the first prospect. A child answered the phone. She didn't understand what Timothy wanted, and then a woman came on the line. Timothy said he was looking for Ben, and the woman said he was at work. Could she help him?

"He sent an email asking to look at our model home," Timothy said.

"Who is this again?"

"Timothy Dugan. I'm with Harcourt Properties. We have a beautiful development going up just outside of town."

The woman said she didn't know why her husband had called. They weren't looking for a new house. And even if they were, that was something she had to be involved in, and since he didn't say a thing about it, she was afraid Timothy had wasted his time. She hung up.

The next few calls didn't yield much. No one was home, so Timothy left messages. His cheerful, peppy voice sounded false, but he kept at it. He made sure to mention the open house. "Bring all your friends," he said. "Get ready for the best time ever!"

He put his phone down and pulled up some pictures he took in the spring. One was good. It was of icicles hanging in one of the gorges. With Photoshop he was able to give the icicles a warm glow, an inner aura, which made them much less somber than in the original shot. He changed the layers and intensity of the colors, creating nine versions of the original. He reviewed the group. There was a progression of mood that didn't follow a logical arc, yet the sequence made sense, somehow.

He opened other photos and played with them, changing the background, then the foreground, so the eye would be drawn wherever he wanted it to go. A couple were of Sam from their early days. In one, she sat under a tree on campus, reading a book. She had just started school. On his days off, he met her there when she was done. On that particular afternoon, they were going to meet Angie later, and Sam said they should just hang out until then.

He focused on her hands as she held the book. The photo clearly showed their size and roughness, but also how gentle they were. He wanted to capture that, and he had, beautifully. He looked through other pictures of her. In every one, she was doing something, reading, writing, standing at the stove, or working in the garden. Most shots didn't show her face, and he wondered about that now. She had a good face, warm and open, yet he chose to focus on the rest of her, always busy.

He reviewed more landscape shots. The first was another sad-looking barn in a dead field under a gray sky. He thought of giving the sky light, just as he had the icicles. He wondered why he was trying to endow the season he loved most with the thing he loved least.

The back door opened, and a moment later Sam stood in the doorway.

"What are you doing?" she asked.

"Hi. Just messing with some pictures I took last winter."

"You missed dinner."

He turned to face her. "I didn't think it was a formal invitation."

"I said it was."

"No, you didn't."

"Read the text again."

He did. It was right there: *come at 6.*

"Sounded like a command performance," he said.

Sam dropped her backpack on the floor and put her hands on her hips.

"They got back from their honeymoon. Alma planned a special dinner to welcome them home. I told you all this a couple of days ago," she said.

She went into the kitchen, then onto the back porch. He saved his work, turned off the computer, and joined her. He expected to find her crying, but her face was dry. She took off her sandals. Her toes were thick and callused. Once, she and Lavinia had gotten pedicures together. Sam came home with pink polish on her nails. That evening, watching TV after dinner, she put her feet in his lap so he could see how soft and smooth they were. He liked the way they felt. Now her heels were rough again, and sometimes scratched him when she moved around in bed.

She registered his presence with a slight relaxing of her shoulders. He wanted to touch her and didn't.

"I'm sorry. I should have remembered about the dinner," he said.

"You forgot because you didn't want to come."

"You're right, I didn't want to be there."

"I wish you came, anyway. It wasn't easy facing it alone."

"Facing what?"

"Their questions. Especially Alma's. She's the nosiest."

"Questions about what?"

She showed him her left hand. The diamond threw brilliant dots of color, enhanced by the setting sun.

"Why did you wear it?" he asked.

"I wanted to see how I liked it. And the idea of the life that went with it."

Timothy said he had a little trouble with that. When she asked him to explain, he said it sounded like she wasn't taking his proposal seriously, that it was something she could take or leave. First, she doesn't want to wear the ring, because she's not thinking about marriage at all, and isn't big on the idea when she does think about it. Then she wears it over to his parents' place, knowing full well what they're going to think it means. She's clearly trying to make up her mind whether to marry him or not.

"So?" she asked.

"So you're turning it into some sort of game. One day you don't want to get married, the next, you slip on this ring to see if you'll feel differently as if the ring itself has the power to change how you feel about the whole thing."

"Is that what you thought when you bought it?"

"No!"

"Come on. It's been at least two years since you even mentioned the word marriage. Then you give me this honking ring. What made you buy it, anyway? I still don't know."

"Because the time was right. I want to marry you. And I think you must want to marry me, too, since you showed the damn thing off to my parents."

Sam laughed.

"You should have seen your mother's face. I can't tell which of us she had more trouble picturing at the altar—you, or me. My money's on you," she said.

Timothy laughed, though he didn't think anything was funny. The alcohol he had earlier was nudging ugly truths into his line of sight. He bought the ring to please his mother. He was a full-grown man, needing Mom's approval.

Sam said his parents were eager to meet Mark when he came back from camp. They were both thrilled at the idea of being grandparents, though they didn't feel old enough for that. They asked her all about him, and she did her best to fill them in, which wasn't easy since they hadn't spent a lot of time together.

The light thinned, and the aroma of a neighbor's barbecue drifted over them. Timothy said he was hungry, and Sam said that was another reason he should have shown up for dinner. He asked if she felt like going out and grabbing a burger.

"I just ate," she said.

"Right."

His parents, particularly Lavinia, asked about Angie. Sam said she and Matt seemed to be doing fine. His connection with that woman was apparently all over, though Sam was doubtful. She said nothing of that over dinner, however.

"You think he's still talking to her?" Timothy asked. He really wanted a burger.

"I think Matt doesn't know right from wrong."

"Someone like that can do a lot of damage."

"I'm afraid he already has."

"You just said Angie was doing fine."

"But their relationship suffered."

You can't carry on with someone else and not cause a big lack of trust, she said, even if you promise to break it off. Then there's the fact that in his state of willful ignorance, Matt was using a typical double standard.

"Why do you say that?" Timothy asked.

"Because if Angie were in touch regularly with a former boyfriend, he wouldn't like it one bit."

That was true. Matt was living on borrowed time. Angie might be a fool for him, but her foolishness had limits. Potter had put a lot of money into The Hole, and if things between Matt and Angie went south, Lavinia would buy Matt out in a New York minute, and then where would he be?

"He needs to get a clue," Timothy said.

"For real."

Sam asked if he wanted a ham sandwich. With a pickle on the side? He said that sounded great.

While Sam was in the kitchen, Timothy sat in one of the porch chairs. The heat of the day had given way to a pleasant coolness which along with gathering clouds suggested rain overnight. He hoped the day of the open house would be sunny because people would feel like getting out and doing something. Then again, on a rainy day, the model home would show well, with its bright, airy spaces.

He thought about Sasha and how she threw herself at him. Why did he allow it? He should have stopped her. Maybe not going as far as she wanted made her mad, and she'd get back at him by telling Jack he was the one to kick things off. She might say he was aggressive and tried to overpower her. Women did things like that, accusing men of going too far when they were the ones who wanted it.

He recalled her story about Jack getting sued. That could be bad for publicity, and bad publicity translated into lost dollars. Harcourt was an idiot for hiring Jack in the first place. Yet, Timothy had a good feeling about him. He was honest and direct, even if his daughter were a slut, though he probably didn't know about that.

His phone buzzed in his pocket. He looked at the number and accepted the call.

"I hope isn't a bad time," Melissa said.

"Just about to sit down to dinner."

"I'll be quick. Mark took a tumble down a trail out there and they're sending him home."

"Is he okay?"

"Yeah. Just a bad sprain, but he can't keep up now."

"Bummer."

"Yeah. His flight gets in tomorrow afternoon. I have to be at work. I don't think I can take time off to go get him. I just started there, and I don't want to be asking for favors so soon."

"You want me to pick him up?"

"Can you? I'll collect him after work."

"Text me the flight info."

"Okay. Thanks."

They hung up.

Timothy didn't like her asking for his time, but he supposed he was going to have to get used to it. Mark was his son. He had to show up when he was needed.

"Who was that?" Sam asked as she handed him the plate and sat down in the other chair. Timothy filled her in.

"Poor kid. He must be disappointed," she said.

"Probably. You'd think they'd take better care of them."

"Anyone can fall, especially if he's not used to hiking on that kind of terrain."

"Yeah."

Timothy ate. The sandwich hit the spot. He wanted another drink and thought he should wait. He needed to gauge Sam's mood. She was watching him and pretending not to, the way she did when she was trying not to show she was upset about something.

"I suppose they wanted to know when the wedding would be," Timothy said.

"Your parents? I told them we didn't know, that you just proposed the other day."

He took her hand. He could feel the sharp points of the diamond against his palm. Lavinia would figure they had no idea how to plan a wedding. She'd try to take charge and he'd have to rein her in. If she didn't take the hint, he'd tell her to lay off, and if *that* didn't work, he'd remind her he was her first child to walk up the aisle, and the first one to have a kid. He had done what was expected of him or was in the process of doing so, which should be plenty for someone who believed in hard lines and narrow paths.

"Do you ever feel like people just want you to live in a box?" he asked.

Sam was quiet for a long moment. She said she knew what he meant by that question, and she guessed why he was asking it, but felt people just wanted you to be happy. There were recognized ways to be happy, things people did and had always done, that seemed the right things to do. This was how traditions got started and took hold. Observing these traditions often made people happy, but sometimes they didn't. Some people weren't made for traditions, or rather, they liked to do things their own way.

"But it's important to keep an open mind. To be able to change your point of view," she said.

"Like about getting married."

"Right. I was certain I would never want to, then thought I should be flexible about the idea, and well, here we are."

"So, we're getting married."

"We are."

"This calls for a drink."

"There's still some white wine left."

Timothy went into the kitchen and poured himself a large glass of bourbon. Then he poured a glass of wine for Sam. He brought the glasses to the screen door. The door handle was hard to operate with the glasses he was carrying. Sam didn't move to help him.

He managed the door and put the glasses on the table. He sat and proposed a toast.

"To us," she said.

"If you toast us, we can't drink."

"Who says?"

"It's a tradition."

"To the future."

"To the future."

They sipped their drinks. He asked if she were happy. She said she was. Would being married change things, she asked. He said he didn't think so, but if so, then only for the better.

It was completely dark then, and the stars blinked as clouds moved in and away.

He told her about Melissa's idea of joint custody. Sam put down her glass.

"I don't know about that," she said.

"Why not?'

"Well, it's a lot, having a twelve-year-old in the house on a regular basis."

"You wanted to have a baby. What's the difference?"

"You have nine months to get used to the idea of a new person in your life. You have time to plan. There's no time, here. And babies are small. They take up less space. They grow slowly, and you can adjust little by little."

She asked when Melissa had first brought up the subject. Timothy said he didn't remember, maybe a couple of weeks ago.

"Why didn't you tell me?"

"I just did."

"No, why didn't you tell me at the time?"

"I don't know. I didn't want to think about it, I guess."

"And then you decided you could think about it."

"Exactly. We're getting married, and planning the future, this seemed like a good time. Why, what difference does it make?"

"None, I guess."

Sam said they should have Mark stay with them for a weekend to see how it went. They could set up a schedule. He could be with them every other week. In a few months, they'd know what it was like.

Timothy said it was a great idea.

They drank. Sam got bitten by a mosquito and said it was time to go in. He said he'd be right there.

He sat, watching the sky. The light from the stars had traveled for millions of years to reach him. He felt like he was traveling, too. Only he had much further to go.

Chapter Fourteen

Timothy got to the airport early and discovered Mark's plane was forty minutes late. He sat in the small waiting area and used his phone to answer some emails. He had nine appointments lined up to show houses. When he mentioned that earlier to Harcourt, Harcourt didn't seem pleased. He and Jack were still arguing about who was going to do the stonework, and also about which drywaller would do a better job. Jack was pushing for highly skilled, qualified people who charged more; Harcourt, as always, wanted to do things on the cheap. When he was able to get a word in, Timothy sided with Jack, which made Harcourt clench his jaw. He probably regretted hiring him. Timothy didn't care. He set aside a chunk of change to protect the company, and he wanted something to show for it. When he had it, he'd tell Harcourt he wanted out, and to find another investor. Let someone else try to convince him that wanting to build crap always comes back to bite you in the butt.

Just before Timothy left for the airport, Harcourt told him his father was coming up from DC tomorrow for the open house. Timothy asked why.

"He wants to see how the construction's shaping up," Harcourt said. Timothy thought even if he inspected the progress at every site, he might not be able to tell a thing unless he knew his two-by-fours from his two-by-sixes. The only completed house was the model home, and the kitchen and bathroom finishes were good. The fixtures were high-end. Behind the walls might be another story. Timothy hoped the water lines were the right size, and the inspector had caught it before, if not. Damn Harcourt anyway.

"He'll be impressed, I'm sure," Timothy said. At that, Harcourt looked happy, or relieved, Timothy couldn't tell, but at least he didn't look like he was about to put his head through a wall.

Melissa texted to say she got an alert the flight was delayed in Buffalo.

What's he doing there? Timothy texted back.

Layover.

Gotcha.

Looks like it's on its way now, though.

Great, thanks!

A couple of minutes passed. A woman stood at the ticket counter, demanding to know why she had to pay for a bag she wanted to check. She was wearing a silk dress and expensive sandals and didn't look like the bag fee would set her back too far.

I really appreciate this, Melissa texted.

No problem.

Let me know if he gives you any trouble.

You betcha.

The board indicating arrivals and departures updated its information. Mark's flight was expected to be on the ground in twenty minutes.

I'm sorry, Melissa texted.

About what?

Everything.

Timothy sighed. What was she trying to do now? Wasn't it enough that he was taking care of her kid?

Their kid.

Jesus.

It hit him all over again that he and Melissa had a child together. Their relationship was never going to be cool and distant. Mark would pull them together just by existing, having things he needed, problems he couldn't solve alone that would take one of them, or both together, to sort out.

The plane landed and Timothy went to the baggage claim where they agreed to meet. People streamed by, talking, not talking, looking at phones, looking around for directions on where to go. Finally, Mark showed up. His left foot was in one of those walking casts. His hair was cut shorter than it had been, and his face and arms were deeply tanned. He didn't smile when he saw Timothy. Instead, he held out his hand, and Timothy shook it.

"Any bags?" Timothy asked.

"Everything's in my backpack."

"I can carry it if you want."

"Nah. I'm cool."

They went slowly toward the parking lot. Timothy asked how the camp had been before he wrecked his ankle. Mark said it was good, though the food sucked. The other kids were weird. They were rich and had been to lots of places, but he got along with them anyway. The thing is, if you let people talk about themselves, they think you're super interested in whatever crap they have to say.

Timothy laughed.

"It sounds bad, but it works," Mark said.

"Did your mom teach you that?"

"Her? No way. She doesn't know how to make friends."

"She doesn't?"

"Well, she doesn't have any, so I guess not."

The heat hit them hard after the coolness of the airport.

After they got in the car, Timothy asked Mark if he were hungry, and Mark said yeah, a little. He was texting on his phone.

"Did you let your mom know you got here safe and sound?" Timothy asked.

"Yup."

"Good."

"She'd flip if I didn't."

"Yeah?"

Mark said one time last year he went home with a friend after school. He was sure he told her about it, but she said he hadn't. Anyway, he was supposed to check in every day, and that day he forgot. His phone was in his backpack and he didn't see it light up with her calls. She panicked, called the school, called the parents of all his friends, and finally the mother of the guy whose house he was at. He thought the whole thing was stupid, and he was mad at her for freaking out like that. The thing was, though, she was crying when he talked to her on the phone.

"Wow," Timothy said.

"Yeah. I didn't give her too much crap after that."

Mark asked about his car, how much it cost, and whether it was fun to drive. He said his grandpa in Buffalo let him drive his Cadillac once, even though he was way underage. They went down a few remote roads outside of town. It was a blast.

"Don't tell my mom," Mark said.

"I won't."

Sam was waiting for them at the house. She greeted Mark warmly and asked how bad his sprain was. He said it was okay. She said she had a chicken sandwich and potato chips ready for him in the kitchen. He went into the kitchen, took a seat at the counter, and ate quickly.

Sam's journal was out on the dining room table, and she told Mark she was going to work a little bit longer, and he could watch television if he wanted. He said he had a book he was going to read if that were okay.

"Awesome!" Sam said.

She looked at Timothy standing idly in the kitchen and asked him if he was all done with work for the day. He said he was. Then he realized he'd be there when Melissa came to get Mark. He'd rather avoid her at the moment, so he told Sam he had some errands to run. He told Mark he'd see him again, soon.

"Cool," Mark said. It looked like the book he was reading was science fiction, judging from the images of laser beams on the cover.

Back in his car, he thought about going down to The Hole. He didn't want to see Matt or Angie, though. He had enough of their drama to last a lifetime. He thought about what Mark had said about Melissa. It sounded as if she hadn't evolved much since college. She certainly was a loner, then. Was she lonely? She had Mark now. And despite what he said about her having no friends, she might make some at work. He could go back to the trailer and make some more calls, make sure the air conditioning in the model home hadn't gone out again, or do any one of a million things that would keep his mind active. None appealed.

He wasn't surprised to find Alma in his mother's kitchen, because she hung out there even when she wasn't cooking. As always, she was reading a dog-eared paperback. She was a dedicated reader and made great use of the downtown Dunston library. When he was a boy, she brought him with her a couple of times. It was from her he learned to love books, though the titles she steered him toward were silly and featured children whose lives were softer than his.

He was drawn to adventure stories, especially gruesome ones that took place in the time of intrepid explorers hacking their way through the Amazon and fleeing from savage headhunters. No one else in his family read except Foster and

Potter, and Potter adopted the habit only after he became sober. Or mostly sober.

"I hear congratulations are in order," Alma said. She put her book face-down on the counter where she was sitting on one of Lavinia's padded high-backed stools.

"Thanks!"

"Quite a time you're having, learning you're a dad, and now planning to get hitched."

"Yup."

"And a new job."

"Full plate."

Alma studied him. She patted her hair, a mass of unflattering tight gray curls.

"Then why do you look so miserable?" she asked.

"I don't."

"Go look in the mirror."

Timothy opened the fridge and helped himself to a bottle of water. He asked if Lavinia were around.

"Hairdressers," Alma said.

Timothy said he wanted to look through some of his old stuff, things he kept from when he was a kid, pictures he might have taken, or papers from school; that sort of junk he hoped Lavinia hadn't thrown away. Alma said there were a bunch of boxes in the hall closet upstairs, and he could help himself, only he had to be sure to put everything back where he found it because she wasn't going to go up there and do it for him.

"I will, I will, don't worry," he said.

The boxes were where Alma said they'd be. The closet was across from a tall window that overlooked the backyard. An empty birdbath stood in the center of a small patio. Timothy couldn't remember there ever being water in it, or birds visiting. In fall it collected leaves; in winter, snow. It was another useless item in a house full of useless items, like the jacuzzi tub Lavinia had put in her bathroom and then never used; or the home theater in the basement where a handful of movies played while each of the kids took their turn hosting friends for a sleepover or birthday party; or the pool table and dartboard in the game room at the back of the house, though Timothy had made good use of it in high school. Chip taught him how to play, more of his grooming Timothy to be the kind of young man Lavinia would be proud of when she never cared how many balls he sank, or how well he knew how to mix drinks. Lavinia was all about practical skills and determination.

Timothy didn't know what he was looking for, just something to show Mark who he was at that age. In a shoebox under several empty photo albums someone must have given him to nurture his growing interest he found some artsy black-and-white snapshots of the local gorges. The slate walls formed layers like shelves. The shot was badly composed, but something was compelling about how one was drawn to the stone and not the water, which was present only in the corner as a grainy white blur. The shoebox held other attempts. He made his siblings sit for him, with caused a lot of complaining and yelling. Foster was the best subject. His silent agitation was palpable in the way he held his hands tightly in his lap. The ones of Angie featured the nose ring and spiked hair she adopted in high school. She was pretty, despite them. He never really thought of her that way before. The twins, sure. They were gorgeous. But Angie had her charm. She grew into herself, he thought. When she wasn't suffering from Matt's idiocy she was calm and centered, the way Timothy wanted to be, too.

There were pictures of Lake Dunston with snow on the shore. Two or three were good. He entered one in a school competition and won third place. No one congratulated him except Alma. And Chip. No one connected to him by blood gave a damn.

He wasn't going to be that way with Mark. He'd show up at every parent-teacher conference, and every awards event, and if he got into sports, he'd show up for all his games. When Mark was the age Timothy was now, he'd be able to say his dad was always there for him.

He set aside a few pictures, put the rest back in the box, put the box away, and went downstairs. He asked Alma if she had an envelope he could use.

"Not much of a letter writer these days, but I can give you a Ziploc if you want."

"Sure, thanks."

She looked at the pictures as she put them in the baggie. She said he was talented, and hoped he was still using his camera from time to time.

"Not as much as I should."

"Well, here you go. We missed you at dinner the other night. I'll get Lavinia to ask you again, and then we can all celebrate properly."

"Sounds good."

As he drove the long way home, he considered how many messages he got from his family when Sam was flipping out about his being late, then again when they learned about Mark. Now he was getting married, and no one had said anything. He was pretty sure Potter and Lavinia would have told everyone, but maybe they hadn't. Wouldn't Sam have talked to Angie about their engagement? Maybe she didn't want to bring it up until things settled down between her and Matt.

Melissa's car, an unassuming Toyota sedan was in front of the house. Her presence made him long to keep driving, but that was a cheap escape. He turned off the engine, got out, smoothed down his hair, stopped briefly on the thinning spot on top, and went in through the back door to find the women at the dining room table drinking wine.

"Hi," Sam said.

"Hi."

"We thought we'd have some wine while we waited for you," Sam said.

"So I see."

"Help yourself, if you want. Or bourbon. Whichever."

"I'm good."

He looked at Mark in the living room. He was still reading.

"Seems like a bad sprain," Timothy said to Melissa.

"That's why they sent him home."

She was wearing a pale blue sleeveless dress with lace around the collar.

Melissa said they should get going. Mark had a doctor's appointment for his ankle. She stood up and hugged Timothy, then she hugged Sam. Timothy told Melissa about the open house on Saturday.

"I'm not in the market, at the moment," she said.

"Bring Mark. Just for a bit. He can meet his grandparents. I'll call them tonight and invite them."

He saw her thinking about it. He told her how to find the building site.

"We'll see how things go," she said.

As she and Mark were through the door, Sam called out she hoped to see them again soon. When Timothy joined her at the table, she asked him if he thought a real estate open house were a great place to introduce Mark to Potter and Lavinia.

"Who cares? I'm not going to get all formal about things."

"I wasn't suggesting you should."

Sam refilled her glass. She told him Mark said he didn't like camp, and that people weren't all that nice. In a way, he was glad when he got hurt, because he wanted to come home. Sam thought from the way he talked that going in the first place was Melissa's idea, not his, despite her saying at lunch he was keen. Sometimes when your parent presents you with something they've already decided you go along with it, or at least pretend you do, in the hope you'll stop hating the idea.

She said when Melissa arrived, she noticed Mark's mood changed. His body tensed. To be honest, they didn't seem all that glad to see each other. They were polite, but not warm. Timothy asked why Sam invited Melissa to hang around if that were the case.

"It seemed like the right thing to do, that's all," she said.

"Sounds to me like you wanted a chance to observe her some more, see if she's a good mother."

"Twenty minutes over a glass of wine wouldn't have told me that."

Timothy told her to tell him the rest of it, whatever it was.

She said there was nothing to tell, except that Melissa was terribly unhappy.

"How do you know?" Timothy asked.

"It's obvious."

"Not to me."

Sam's expression said his powers of observation weren't anything to brag about. He asked if Melissa said anything specific.

"Only that she wasn't sure she did the right thing, coming back here," Sam said.

"She's been back awhile. Why wonder about it now?"

"I'm just telling you what she said."

Sam sipped her wine. It was so unlike her to drink during the day.

"It must have been hard for her to reach out to you. And to realize how much she still cares for you. Her feelings are all in a tizzy, and she's lost," Sam said.

"Doesn't look lost to me."

"She hides it well."

"Why are you taking her side?"

Sam stood, took her glass to the sink, and poured the contents down the drain. Her hair had slipped from the silver clip holding it all up on the back of her head.

"It's always a question of sides with you, isn't it? What if there are no sides? What if there are just people, trying to find a way to be happy and figure things out?"

She had a noticeable slur as she spoke. He approached and put his hand gently on her shoulder.

"Just tell me what's bothering you," he said.

"Nothing."

"I don't think that's true."

She turned. The color in her cheeks was redder now. Her eyes were glassy, yet full of pain.

"I just don't know where I'm supposed to fit into all of this. I keep trying to figure it out," she said.

"You're my fiancée. That's how you fit in."

Melissa would have seen the ring. There was no way she could have missed it. That's why she was unhappy. Timothy was going to marry someone else when she wanted him to marry her.

Sam asked him what he was thinking.

"That you're a little drunk," he said.

"I hope you don't mind."

"I don't."

They talked about what they'd do for dinner. Sam wanted to go out. She was feeling cooped up. Timothy said there was a new brewpub on the Commons. He thought it might give The Hole a run for its money. Should they go and check it out?

Sam said sure, she'd go change, and splash some water on her face.

"Thank you," he said.

"For what?"

"For always trying to do the right thing."

She gazed at the floor for a moment, and the look in her eyes said she thought doing the right thing was a stupid waste of time.

Later, when they got in the car, Sam asked what was in the shoebox. He told her. She said it was a lovely idea and was sure Mark would appreciate seeing what he was into at that age.

But it was who he was now that Timothy wanted him to know. And that meant spending a lot of time together, without Melissa and Sam around. He should wrap things up with Harcourt sooner rather than later and take a few weeks off before Mark started school. He wondered what he did while Melissa was at work. He'd find out and make some plans.

Chapter Fifteen

Timothy woke full of joy. Sam was still in bed, another anomaly. The sky held clouds and the breeze through the open window had a sweet, cool touch.

He dreamed about being on the shore of a lake watching the waves reflect light. His camera hung around his neck, and he lifted it to look through the viewfinder. What he saw there was a different scene, a place he didn't recognize. The lake had been replaced by an open field with an orchard. When he looked again, the lake had returned.

He lay, loving the weight of his limbs on the warm sheets and the steady rise and fall of Sam's breathing. The changing scenes were his brain reminding him of impermanence, something his love of history reinforced. The book on Caesar was finished and he began a biography of Mathew Brady. What it would have taken to photograph the dead at Antietam, all the dead on all the battlefields everywhere? Courage, of course, and a strong stomach. But also something more. A drive to create a record for the future, one that spoke for itself simply, without propaganda, and the need to persuade. All his life he watched people trying to impress others to get what they needed. Women looking pretty; men acting cocky and brave; it was all a play written long ago. People were afraid to live the truth, afraid of their own feelings. But not Sam. She was genuine, honest, and open. She had no secrets, no airs or pretenses. He admired that about her and adored her for it. Proposing to her was the first really smart thing he'd done in a long time.

She stirred and rolled away from him. She stretched. Her foot brushed along his leg and her eyes snapped open. He watched her face. For a moment she seemed not to know where she was, which meant she was sleeping deeply. As her face calmed she blinked a couple of times, and the rise and fall of her golden lashes was magical. He picked up her hand and put his thumb on the diamond. The stone was cold, her flesh was warm. Everything about Sam was a study in opposites. She was physically strong yet mild-mannered. She was kind to others, and hard on herself. Poetry had stolen her heart, yet she was always happy with plain, ordinary things. She said once Shaker furniture was her ideal.

She got up and pulled on her flannel bathrobe, one she had for years. He'd buy her a new one. And some new clothes. She'd say her old stuff was fine, but she'd be glad to have them. He wouldn't go overboard. Just a couple of shirts. She always looked good in green.

"Do we still have that espresso maker we got a couple of years ago?" he asked.

"What? I don't know. Why?"

"I'm in the mood for a really strong cup of coffee."

"Oh, okay, well I think I know where it is."

She stared down at him. She smiled.

"You always look your best, first thing in the morning," she said.

"I was just going to say the same thing about you."

He roosted in bed while she rummaged in the kitchen for the espresso maker. She must have found it because soon there was a glorious smell of coffee that was more intense than usual. He sat up and swung his legs over the side of the bed. A minute later he was in the kitchen with his arms around her, kissing her neck.

"Cut it out, I have coffee to pour," she said.

"I love you, Sam Clark."

"I love you, too, Timothy Dugan."

She handed him a small cup of espresso. He took it to the table and sat. There were a handful of dandelions in the backyard grass. He'd pull them before heading over to the building site, though Sam usually did that. He watched her in the kitchen getting a cup of espresso for herself.

"Will you keep your name, or take mine?" he asked.

"Do you think the world needs another Dugan?"

"Probably not."

She joined him. She held up her left hand and said she was already as traditional as she was going to get.

He asked her where she wanted to go for a honeymoon. She sipped her coffee. Loose strands of hair fell charmingly across her cheek.

"We could take that trip to Maine," she said.

"Oh, to hell with Maine. Let's go someplace really great."

"Like where?"

"England."

"Are you serious?"

He said he was. He had money. What better way to spend some of it than to take his beautiful bride on a beautiful trip?

"What about work?" she asked.

He put his cup in the saucer and said it wasn't going too great.

"What? You've only been there a couple of weeks," she said, though she didn't sound angry or alarmed, just curious.

He explained Harcourt was a bad businessman, and the contractor, Jack, had a history of using substandard materials. The current project would probably turn out all right, and he'd make some money, but it wasn't something he could see himself doing for the long term.

She said if he were going to be unemployed for a while, they shouldn't plan a big expensive trip. He said he had enough to live on for a couple of years, at least.

"Really?" she asked.

He told her the balance in his account.

"I had no idea," she said.

"I got it when Chip died."

"That was generous of him."

She sat, with her big hands around her cup. She could crush it if she wanted to, he thought.

"I told you about the money I got from my father," she said.

"I remember."

"And you didn't tell me about yours."

"I didn't think you cared."

"I don't."

"So, what's the problem?"

She leaned back in her chair. She looked down at her blue placemat. His was red, part of a set they got their first summer at the Dunston Farmers' Market.

She didn't care about money, she said. She grew up without it. What she got from her father she was grateful for, of course. She tried to avoid looking at it as compensation for her childhood, though in fact, it was exactly that. But she had it now, and most of it was invested. She took her share of their modest expenses from it, as he knew, but didn't want to touch the rest of it, not yet, anyway. The point is she was open about what she had when they got together. On his side of the equation was this house, given to him by Chip, which he told her about. But the money, she didn't know about that.

"So?"

"It changes my understanding of you, of your situation."

"What are you talking about?"

"When a person has that kind of money, taking a job or leaving a job doesn't have the same gravity. A hefty bank account makes choices less important because there are fewer consequences."

He was beginning to see what she was getting at. His decision to leave the GAP didn't demonstrate the degree of courage she assumed it did because if the thing with Harcourt failed, he'd be okay financially, regardless.

"You knew I had to guarantee fifty thousand dollars for Harcourt's business," Timothy said.

"No, I didn't know that."

"I told you."

"No, you didn't."

It was Lavinia he told, not Sam. He wasn't sure why he confused the two.

He asked her to please boil this down for him because he needed to get ready for the open house.

"I think I've been clear. I didn't know you had that kind of money. I would like to have known, but I know now," she said. He could see he wasn't going to get anything more out of her.

He said he was going to get showered, then head on over to the model home. Things were going to kick off over there around one. She could come early if she wanted.

"Okay," she said.

After his shower, he stood in the closet and rejected one shirt after another. He settled on a long-sleeved pale purple cotton with white buttons. Standing in front of the full-length mirror that leaned against the wall he thought he looked too eager. To tone down that image, he exchanged his khakis for blue jeans. As he debated whether he'd wear lightweight socks or just slide his bare feet into his loafers, he heard Sam talking on the phone.

"Isn't it next Saturday?" she asked. There was a pause. "I don't why I got that mixed up. There are only so many Saturdays in July." She chuckled. "Okay, at seven. I have something on this afternoon, and I don't know when it will wind down, but I'll be there." Another pause. "Oh, I think she is, too. One of my idols. Okay, then. Bye."

He went into the kitchen. Whatever the conversation had been about, it pleased her, judging from the little smile she had. When she saw him watching her, she said, "The poetry reading's tonight."

"Who was that?"

"Steven."

"Who?"

"Professor Wells. You remember."

"Right."

Sam said Melanie Sawyer was coming to read at Kensington Hall. Timothy nodded. He asked her if she thought his shirt were all right.

"Yeah, you look great. Oh, you cut yourself shaving." She pointed to his chin. He returned to the mirror. The cut had stopped bleeding. Still, he wished he hadn't done it. He should give up shaving for a while. He had a beard for a while back in college which earned him various nicknames. Castro stuck until he told the frat brothers to leave him the hell alone. A beard would make him look distinguished, more than it had before. He was too young back then to carry it off.

When he got to the building site, there was a car he didn't recognize parked up by the model home. He asked Harcourt who it belonged to, and he said the caterer was there, getting ready. He was in a bad mood. Another house failed inspection, something about the foundation not being poured correctly. As he explained the situation, and Timothy started to speak, Harcourt held up his hand. This one was a fair mistake, not an attempt to cut corners.

"Fair mistake, how?" Timothy asked.

"The concrete guy is new. Didn't know what he was doing. I've got someone else up there, now."

Timothy was sure Harcourt approved using someone inexperienced specifically to save money, but he wasn't going to get into that. He said he was heading up to the model home to make sure everything was ready to rock and roll.

"Oh, when does your dad get here?" he asked.

"He's not coming."

"That's too bad."

Harcourt stared gloomily at his computer.

Timothy walked up the hill under full sun, since the morning clouds and coolness had vanished. Adele was in the kitchen, lining up glassware and cutlery. There was a long, woven piece of fabric on the counter and a vase of lovely iris and roses. Another floral arrangement was on the kitchen table. Small stacks of information sheets about the house were scattered throughout so people could look at them wherever they happened to be.

"The food arrives at twelve-thirty," Adele said. She wiped each champagne glass with a cloth, held it to the light to inspect it, then set it gently in the row she established. She did the same thing to each knife and fork. Timothy asked how she got into catering.

"I always liked to cook. Well, not cook so much as entertain. We don't have any children, so my husband was the beneficiary of my passion. That's an odd way to put it, isn't it?" she laughed, enjoying a private memory. Her hair was dyed red. The white roots showed. Timothy wondered if she minded. He guessed she didn't. She was overweight, but not badly, and gave the impression of being an easy-going, happy person. He envied her, which made him feel odd.

She went on. She gave a lot of dinner parties for her husband's colleagues and their spouses. Their house became the group's favorite gathering place. When she was first married, she couldn't find her way around a kitchen at all, and her husband was nice about it, though she could tell he wished she'd get up to speed, at least on the basics, like how to make toast without burning it. Yeah, she was that clumsy. She worked as a secretary in the engineering department, and when she got home for the day, tired as she was, she always had the energy to cook. Well, time passed as it always does, and her husband was promoted to full professor, then to chairman of the department, and she was able to quit. There were people in her circle, oddly quite a number of women, who thought she was stupid for not working. Don't rely on your husband's income, they said. You don't know what will happen. Meaning, he might leave her and where would she be then? But where would she be, even if she had a job? She wanted to become the best cook she could be, a chef, even, but that required a stint in someone else's professional kitchen. Which she did, over at Madeleine's, Timothy must know it.

"I do. It's great," he said and looked at his watch.

"I'm keeping you."

"No, it's fine. I'll just walk around the place, make sure everything's good."

"You need toilet paper in the powder room."

"Oh, okay. Thanks for the heads up."

Timothy looked in the cabinet under the power room sink and found it empty. The pantry in the kitchen was also empty. Everything was empty. He called down to Harcourt, who told him he'd have to go and pick some up.

The sky blazed as he drove. His bare feet stuck to the insides of his shoes. He'd spend a fair amount of time on his feet at the open house, and he'd have blisters by the end of the day.

He changed course and went home for a pair of socks. Sam wasn't there. He tried to remember what she said she was doing that morning and couldn't. After he got into his socks, and back into his shoes, he went into the bathroom, checked the linen closet, and took the large package of toilet paper Sam just got at the store. He left a couple of rolls on the shelf so they wouldn't run out themselves. Then he got back in the car and returned to the open house to find Jack and Sasha in the kitchen talking to Adele.

"What are you guys doing here?" Timothy asked Jack.

"Sasha wanted to take a look. Another day with nothing to do, it seems, which is why I keep telling her to get a job."

"I told you, I tried," Sasha said. They weren't really arguing. Their tone was friendly enough.

Sasha eyed Timothy coolly, yet with a touch of humor. Timothy appreciated again how pretty she was. He stocked each bathroom with one roll of toilet paper. Then he realized he needed to put out soap and hand towels, too. Sam didn't answer until the third ring. When he asked where she was, she said she was taking a walk with Lavinia. He told her he needed her to pick up some things for the open house.

"Your mom wants to talk to you, hold on," Sam said and the phone changed hands.

"What's wrong?" Lavinia asked.

"Nothing. I just need Sam to swing by the store and grab some soap and towels for this thing."

"Oh. Well, I have plenty of spare everything. Either I'll send her off with it, or bring it myself."

"If you bring it yourself, get here early. As in, before it starts."

"Didn't plan very well, did you?"

"I have to go."

"I'm sorry, I shouldn't have said that."

Timothy paused and considered his mother's apology. Lavinia never apologized. He asked her if she were all right. She sighed a deep, ragged sigh. She said she was going to go home and take a long bath before coming to the open house. She gave the phone back to Sam.

"What's going on with my mother?" he asked.

"I'll tell you later."

"Okay. And thanks."

Timothy turned around and discovered Sasha watching him. Jack left while he was on the phone, and Adele was on her way out. She said the food was due at the trailer any minute, and she'd be back in a flash.

When they were alone, Sasha asked him to show her the rest of the house.

"Okay, well first take off your shoes," Timothy said.

"Huh?"

There was a basket of disposable slippers by the front door for people to put on because shoes marked up the floor. She did as he asked and removed her sandals. Her feet were small and slender. The nails were painted green. He kicked off his loafers and saw his big toe protruding from a hole he didn't know was there. He moved fast to get the slippers on, but the pair he grabbed was too small. They were supposed to be one-size-fits-all. Harcourt, who bought them just yesterday on his way in, must have gotten someone's close-out inventory. With another pair that fit well enough, he asked her to note the inlay tile inside the front door, and the light fixture directly overhead. They were elegant yet subtle, didn't she agree?

"You got it, Chief," she said.

He asked her to admire the coat closet in the front hall. "Super convenient for guests," he said.

Though the temporary table in the dining room seated eight people, a larger one that could accommodate twelve would be no problem. As to the window coverings, Timothy recommended going for the higher-priced plantation shutters, like the ones installed here. They did a beautiful job filtering the light.

Sasha bit her nails on her right hand. Then she pulled out her phone and scrolled through her messages. Her jaw tightened as she read one.

"An admirer?" Timothy asked.

"To hear him tell it." Her tone was sarcastic. She must have guys lined up, waiting, letting themselves get strung along, Timothy thought.

He showed her the master bedroom and bath, praising the large closets and soaking tub. In the kitchen, he pointed out the wine cooler in which Adele had thoughtfully placed several bottles of good French champagne. Sasha suggested they open one.

"Not a good idea," Timothy said. He talked about the pot filler installed in the tile backsplash over the six-burner range, then said most people went with a four or five-burner, because you had to have a good-sized family to justify having six, but some people wanted the best of everything, even if they seldom used it. Sasha removed a bottle from the cooler and had the cork out before Timothy could object.

"Where did you learn how to do that?" he asked.

"I used to tend bar."

"You could have gotten a summer job doing that easily enough."

"Dad won't let me. Says it's not a good place for a young woman."

The pieces fell into place. Jack was overly protective, so Sasha acted like the bad girl. She poured champagne into two glasses and handed him one. He figured it wouldn't hurt him.

Besides, if a prospect showed up now, it wouldn't look so bad, having a pretty woman drinking champagne. She touched her glass to his and drank. She put the glass on the quartz countertop and leaned in for a long kiss Timothy didn't resist.

He stepped back.

"This isn't going to happen," he said.

"It just did."

"And now it's over."

"What's wrong with you, anyway?"

"I'm engaged."

"Why don't we go break in that nice king-sized bed? Consider it a last hurrah before the chains descend."

"Forget it."

"You're thinking about it, I can tell."

"It would be impossible not to think about it. But thinking is all that's going to happen."

She leaned toward him again and he put his hand on her shoulder to hold her still. She shrugged and turned away. She finished her glass. She rinsed it out before leaving it in the sink.

"Well, can't blame me for trying. You're one tasty dude," she said. She went to the front door and exchanged the slippers for her sandals. She said she was heading back to the trailer. She was going to cruise with her dad on a couple of errands.

"Okay, then," Timothy said.

"Good luck today."

Alone, he took his drink into the living room and sat on the couch. It was upholstered in suede or fake suede, and he handled his glass carefully so it wouldn't spill. A girl like Sasha could get herself in a lot of trouble, by acting like that. But then, she'd have her fun doing it, wouldn't she? He closed his eyes. The air conditioning system hummed gently. Several sites away a staple gun punctuated the silence. The crew would charge overtime for working on a weekend. Timothy was surprised Harcourt authorized that, but then maybe he thought it would look good to buyers and underscore the seriousness of the project.

He took his empty glass into the kitchen and put it in the sink. Then he put the half-full champagne bottle in the fridge. He used the bathroom and made sure his nails were clean. Adele returned, carrying three large flat boxes of food. She was winded. She said she was a dummy for not driving her car down and back. She didn't know why thought she didn't need it. Timothy took the boxes from her and said he would have been happy to come down and help her. She thanked him and said he could help her now if he liked.

They arranged the food on white china platters. There was smoked salmon, crostini, deviled eggs, vegetables and dip, miniature quiches, barbecued chicken wings, slices of watermelon and cantaloupe, a bowl of strawberries, chocolate brownies, white chocolate truffles, and bite-sized chocolate chip cookies. Timothy helped himself to salmon, two eggs, several cookies, and a handful of strawberries. There was no garbage container in the kitchen. The stagers should have brought in one of those snazzy stainless-steel ones. Timothy phoned Harcourt and explained the problem.

"Jesus. Okay, I'll get the guys to put a large rubber container outside the back door. People will just put down their crap when they're done with it, so keep an eye out and toss it when you need to. We've got two wastebaskets down here. Put one in the powder room and the other in the master bath."

He asked Timothy why he hadn't thought of this before. Timothy said he assumed the stagers would take care of it. Harcourt seemed to find that a reasonable explanation.

"Can you bring them up?" Timothy asked.

"Me? No, I'm working on something."

"Hold on."

Timothy asked Adele if she'd go get the wastebaskets from Harcourt. She said she'd be glad to, and left. He told Harcourt she'd be there in a minute. Harcourt said okay. He paused.

"Hello?" Timothy said.

"What happened up there with Sasha?"

"Nothing. Why?"

"Come on. I could see she was frosted about something."

"I assume you're alone in the trailer right now."

"Yeah, they took off."

Timothy said again he didn't know what Harcourt was talking about. Harcourt said Sasha had put the moves on him a while back, while Jack was up at one of the building sites, no less. They had sex on the couch.

"Are you kidding me?" Timothy asked.

"Why not?"

"Because she's, I don't know, young."

"She's twenty-two."

"What if Jack came back while you were at it?"

"That's what made it fun, wondering if he would."

"You're insane."

"No. I just hadn't gotten laid for a while. But anyway, she's a weird chick, so I advise you to steer clear."

Timothy was honest about what had happened. Harcourt said not taking her up on her suggestion to borrow the master bedroom probably earned him her undying hate.

"Girl's got an ego, let me tell you," Harcourt said. He said he had to put the phone down because Adele was outside and he needed to give her the wastebaskets. After a minute, he picked up his phone and resumed. He tried to see Sasha after that, and she didn't want anything to do with him. She wasn't into dating, she told him, just sex. And she made it clear the sex had to be on her terms only, which meant she was the one to make the advance.

Timothy saw Adele huffing her way up the road. He told Harcourt he had to go. When he hung up, he went out and took the wastebaskets from her.

"I'll be as thin as a rail in no time if I keep this up," she said cheerfully. She said she hoped he'd knock 'em dead and would be back in a couple of hours to clean up.

Sam arrived with soap and towels. The towels were Christmas-themed, which Timothy said was all wrong. Sam said it was all Lavinia could find, and no one would care. The soap was from the farmers' market and smelled strongly of lavender and spice. Sam put everything where it belonged, then returned to the kitchen and admired the food, but didn't help herself to any.

Soon, the place was full of people, all realtors there for the food and drink. Several of them had met Harcourt recently and asked if he'd put in an appearance. Timothy said probably, then realized Harcourt would be there already if he were coming. Some made an effort to get to know Timothy personally, at least to the extent of asking him how he got interested in property development, and what he did before that. Most were impressed he attended the university, which was consistent with Timothy's experience that a degree from an Ivy League school carried weight. Everyone admired the house and spoke well of it, but most thought it was priced too high. Timothy gently disagreed. He did his research. He was expecting a quick sale, even an all-cash offer. One woman, with prominent jowls and bags below her eyes, said that kind of buyer wasn't looking to Dunston much these days. Things were happening in Syracuse, though, even Buffalo. Again, Timothy politely disagreed, though he didn't know, one way or another. As they trickled out, Lavinia arrived. She went straight to the kitchen, poured herself a glass of wine, though Sam offered to, and sat down on one of the counter stools. She drank and picked at the smoked salmon on crostini.

Timothy greeted her and asked why she looked upset.

She put her glass on the counter. The rim bore a trace of her pink lipstick.

"Your father came home stinking last night. The first time in a long while, and he apologized, of course. Some people he knew came into the bar, and he just had to have a drink with them. And one became many. Matt drove him home. I don't know why he didn't cut him off, but then, that's not his job, is it? He's not a babysitter. Neither am I. I could smell him from across the room when he opened the door, and I told him he was sleeping elsewhere. He didn't argue, didn't fuss."

Sam said she didn't think Potter would make a habit of it.

"No, I'm sure he won't. He's good at keeping himself under control. Until he permits himself to slip. It's the permitting part that's the problem," Lavinia said.

Timothy was surprised by how deeply upset Lavinia was. He thought by now she'd be used to Potter's lapses, especially after living with him when they were a daily thing.

He looked at his watch. It was getting late. Everyone who was going to show already had. He collected a pile of business cards, so from that standpoint, the event had gone well. He would follow up with every person who came. Yet, he was disappointed. Because Melissa hadn't come.

"Guess you'll have to wait to meet your grandson," he said to Lavinia.

"Oh, that's all right. This isn't the best place for a thing like that. I'll have everyone over to the house, once I sort out this thing with your father."

Timothy didn't see what there was to sort out. His dad screwed up, that's all.

Adele returned and asked if she could start putting things away. Timothy said she could, and the food was delicious.

"Thanks so much!" Adele said. Lavinia poured herself a second glass of wine. Timothy looked at Sam.

"Let me drive you home. Timothy can follow us," Sam said.

"You're afraid I'm under the influence?" Lavinia asked, but her tone was whimsical, not angry.

"I think you could use some company on the drive, that's all," Sam said.

Lavinia's eyes brimmed with affection as she looked at Sam. "You're wonderful, you know that?" she asked.

"I do."

"Even if he never tells you."

"He tells me."

Timothy went into the downstairs powder room to collect the wastebasket. In the master bedroom, he saw someone had sat on the bedspread. Sasha came to mind. He hoped she'd make herself scarce for the rest of the summer.

Sam and Lavinia had left when he returned. He didn't think he'd been gone that long. Adele asked him to please keep her in mind for any other events he might need a caterer for. He promised to and showed her out.

He walked through the house, checked all the windows, and then turned off the air conditioning. The sudden quiet was startling. He stood before the picture window and looked at the lake, shimmering in the distance. The sun was fierce and made the water a painful shade of blue. He went out, locked the front door, walked back to his car, and headed for his mother's to pick up Sam. He hoped Lavinia vented enough about her problems. He wanted to enjoy what was left of the afternoon. He'd head down to The Hole and have a couple of cold ones while Sam went to her poetry reading. That sounded like an excellent idea. A most excellent idea, indeed.

Chapter Sixteen

What he remembered: Matt telling him he had enough; someone taking his phone and calling Sam; her guiding him to the car without a word of recrimination; and the dread he'd hear it all later, in the morning, which it was then. He was alone in bed. The house was silent. The light around the blinds suggested a fierce, rising heat. It was the last weekend in July, and summer would gather strength during August. He didn't know if he could bear it.

Sam was in the yard, watering the plants with the hose. She stood before the hydrangea, then aimed the hose at a pair of rhododendrons that looked sickly despite her tending and fussing over them, then to a row of potted impatiens and begonias. Timothy turned away, swallowed a couple of Tylenol, got himself some coffee, and dug his phone out of the pocket of his jeans, which Sam had thoughtfully folded and left on his side of the dresser.

There was a voice message from Melissa. He finished his coffee before listening to it.

"Timothy, I didn't pick up last night because I was busy. I silenced my phone after the fifth call. There need to be boundaries here. I don't think we have anything to talk about, except Mark. When you sort this out, you're welcome to call me. During the daytime."

The evening came into focus. He went down to The Hole in a good mood. Matt was in a good mood, too. Even Angie had a smile for him. They both apologized for not making it to the open house. Things had been busy at the bar all day. Timothy said it was no big deal, they would have been bored, anyway. He watched Matt and Angie interact from the safety of his barstool. Angie pecked Matt's cheek as she collected Timothy's beer. Matt didn't pick up his phone once. Maybe what's-her-name finally got the message. Thinking that made Timothy feel even better. He liked having put pressure on Matt to straighten up.

Time passed, and the sunny mood gave way to gloom. He was lonely and wished Sam hadn't gone to that stupid poetry reading. She didn't like hanging out at The Hole, and he never got why. It was a pleasant place to be. You could talk to people or not. There was never any pressure.

Angie was at his elbow, saying she didn't think another round was a good idea. He disagreed. She stood firm. He told her to shut up. That was when Matt picked up his phone from the top of the bar and started looking for Sam's number. Angie took the phone from him and made the call. Timothy didn't remember Angie's exact words, only that he grabbed the phone out of her hand. Then Sam was there, asking if he paid his bill.

"Do you need to use the bathroom before we go?" she asked him. He did. He remembered being in the car after that, then being in the bedroom with Sam taking off his jeans.

He went outside now, into the yard, and called her name.

"Sleeping Beauty," she called back. She wasn't mad. He asked where his car was, and she said Angie drove it over to their place last night. All he had to do was call her up and say she could bring it over when she wanted. Or Sam could drive him over. Either way.

"I really tied one on. That was stupid. Guess I just lost track of myself, there," he said. The coffee he sipped was delicious.

Sam approached. Her straw hat shaded her face, and her sunglasses obscured her eyes. She removed her gardening gloves, then twisted the engagement ring so that the diamond was in the right place. He hadn't realized it was too big. She never said.

"What time did you get me, anyway?" he asked.

"Around eight. I got home and was about to text you to see where you were when Angie called."

He asked her how the reading was.

"What? Oh, it was great! Very inspiring," she said.

She removed her hat and wiped the sweat from her brow with the back of her hand. She tossed her hat onto the porch.

"Steven thinks my stuff is just as good, but I don't agree," she said.

Timothy didn't know her professor was so familiar with her work, but then he'd have to be, wouldn't he?

She said there was a writers' conference in a couple of weeks over in Vermont. Steven thought he could score her an extra ticket. She told him she'd pay him for it, she didn't want him to cover the cost, himself.

"Writers' conference?" Timothy asked.

"At Middlebury College. Some big names will be there. He might be able to get me a manuscript consultation, or at least a written critique."

"You have a manuscript?"

"The thing I've been working on."

"Oh, of course."

He asked how long she'd be gone. She said just a couple of days, though the conference ran for a week. She didn't want to be away that long.

"You don't have to stick around, just to keep an eye on me, you know. Last night, notwithstanding," he said. The coffee in his mug was cold now.

"I know." She went past him, into the kitchen, and splashed water on her face. She said Lavinia had invited Melissa and Mark over to her place around three.

"What, today?" he asked through the screen door.

"Yeah."

"Short notice."

"She's like that."

"She should have consulted me."

"Well, you were asleep, so she consulted me. Don't go if you don't want to."

"Are you going?"

"Yes."

"What time, again?" he asked.

"Around three."

"Okie Dokie."

For the get-together, Timothy dressed down in torn jeans and an old 49ers T-shirt. Sam put on a skirt and a sleeveless blouse. She wore the silver beaded necklace he bought her and put her hair up with silver hair clips. He told her she looked great. At the last minute, she sprayed herself with perfume. It made his nose itch and his eyes burn, though he said nothing of it.

Melissa and Mark were already at Lavinia's. Everyone was out back on the brick patio. Potter showed Mark around the yard. Mark didn't limp as badly as he did the other day, though he still had the walking cast on his foot and ankle. Melissa and Lavinia were chatting pleasantly. Melissa's face stiffened when she saw Timothy. Then she smiled at Sam.

"I was just saying, yesterday I felt I couldn't possibly be a grandmother, but today, I'm absolutely thrilled," Lavinia said. Potter and Mark walked over from the azalea hedge they were looking at.

"Your boy's got quite an interest in plants, did you know that?" Potter asked Timothy.

"I didn't."

Timothy and Mark looked at each other.

"Great shirt," Mark said.

"Thanks."

Potter told Timothy to grab himself a beer if he wanted. He was sticking with iced tea, himself. Timothy said iced tea sounded great.

He helped himself to an empty lounge chair next to the one Mark claimed. He had a Game Boy in his hands and was clicking away madly. Melissa told him to put it away. He didn't move. When she asked him again, he glared at her.

"Or I take it, and you don't get it back," she said.

He put it in his lap.

Lavinia said Mark's resemblance to Timothy was positively uncanny. It took her back, remembering Timothy at that age. Potter agreed, meeting Mark was a real trip down memory lane. Timothy wished he could go inside, find some vodka, and spike his glass of tea.

"Is it weird for you to meet all these relatives, all at once?" Sam asked Mark.

Mark shrugged. Then he said it wasn't really. He saw his other grandparents lots of times.

Lavinia asked Mark if he missed them.

"No," he said, and everyone laughed.

As people talked, Timothy relaxed. He knew there wouldn't be many of these family get-togethers as time went on, and Mark was in school. Lavinia just had to do her thing and show everyone she was in control. Well, maybe that wasn't fair. He was sure her interest in Mark was genuine.

Melissa asked Sam if she were at the poetry reading last night.

"Yeah, were you there, too?" Sam asked.

"I was. I thought I saw you in the back."

They paused, and Sam shifted in her chair.

"I was with my professor. He's also my thesis advisor," Sam said.

"But you're an undergraduate, right?"

"It's an honors thesis."

Melissa asked what it was on, and Sam explained about her poetry collection. Timothy tuned out.

Potter told Mark about his other aunts and uncles, Foster, Angie, and the twins down in New York. He said they'd all be around over Christmas, though of course Foster and Angie lived there in town.

"Foster's off camping with a friend this weekend, and Angie's down at The Hole," Lavinia told Mark. Mark barely registered her comment, but he didn't look like he was having a terrible time either, just waiting until he could go home and get back on his Game Boy.

Alma appeared at the kitchen door and asked if she should whip up something to eat. She had a package of pork chops she didn't want to waste. How did that sound? Timothy called back that he was starving. Sam looked at him sharply and said they hadn't planned to stay for dinner.

"Why not?" he asked her.

"I have some work I wanted to finish."

"Do it later."

"I can't."

Everyone else stopped talking. Sam told the group she was in the middle of a really exciting poem, and she didn't want to be away from it too long. Timothy said that was the most ridiculous thing he ever heard. If her creative juices were flowing before, they would again easily enough.

"Oh, what do you know about it?" Lavinia asked. Her tone was teasing and light.

"Nothing."

A few minutes later, Timothy said he had to use the bathroom and went into Chip's former study, where Lavinia kept her top-shelf liquor. He poured some vodka into his tea, then went into the kitchen to see if Alma needed help. He told her it would be easier for Mark to visit with his family if he weren't around. He seemed to make him nervous.

"Or, he makes you nervous," Alma said and smashed a peeled clove of garlic on the cutting board. He sat on a counter stool and watched her work.

Mark wandered in and said he was thirsty. Alma got him a glass of water. He drank it down in one go and gave the glass back to her.

"This is a cool house," he said. Timothy offered to show him around. Mark said Potter was setting up a croquet game, but maybe later?

"Sure. Go have fun with Granddad," Timothy said.

Timothy freshened his drink with more tea from the refrigerator and more vodka from the study. Alma didn't ask about his temporary absence, but she did look at him closely when he returned. He was glad she didn't try to engage him in conversation. He said he should probably get back.

Potter and Mark played croquet while Sam stood nearby, offering words of encouragement. Timothy took the empty seat next to Melissa. He asked her why she wasn't playing, too. She said she just didn't feel like it at the moment. He said he was sorry he called her so many times last night. He couldn't remember what had been on his mind. He'd be honest—he had a little too much to drink. He hoped she understood. She nodded. She looked miserable.

Lavinia asked Alma to set dinner up on the picnic table so everyone could help themselves when and if they wanted. Timothy ate quickly; Melissa merely picked. When Timothy said she didn't seem hungry, she said she never ate much.

Mark, however, was a different story. He enjoyed Alma's chops and potatoes but passed on the salad. Melissa said he wasn't much for healthy food.

"That might change," Timothy said. He put his plate on the grass next to his chair.

Potter offered Mark another game of croquet. Sam wanted to play, too, and needed a partner. She asked Timothy and Melissa if either wanted to join her, and both declined. Lavinia went into the house to look for some family photo albums, and Sam returned to the yard to watch Potter and Mark play. Timothy noted how Potter interacted with Mark. He was friendly, but not overbearing. He admired how easily he talked to him. Potter had the gift of meeting people on their own terms. Sam did, too. Just then, she was cheering Mark for the swing he just made. Mark took a bow and grinned. Timothy saw himself, then, as the boy he might have been with different parents or the kind of people Lavinia and Potter had become.

"Look what we did," Melissa said, meaning Mark.

"Yeah."

He waited for her to say something else and didn't mind when she didn't. Then she asked him about Harcourt, if he liked working with him, if he saw his future there. Timothy was candid about his concerns. He glided into his interest in photography, which seemed to be resurging at the moment. He wondered if there were a way to combine that with working in real estate. He didn't want to take pictures of houses, though, that seemed too boring. She said he could ask former clients if he could return a few months after a sale and take some shots of their dining room, or wherever they normally ate. An album of dining rooms would be interesting because it would show a cross-section of people's tastes, backgrounds, and cultural heritage. Some people would refuse and need persuading, but she bet most would like the idea of having their things on display. Buying a home made you proud of what you did with your life.

He asked if she hoped to own a home, one day. She said she didn't think she'd ever be able to. He asked if her parents might help. She said she didn't know.

He told her about the money he inherited from his late stepfather. What if he bought her a house? If she were uncomfortable with the idea, she could pay him rent. After a few years, and with her permission, he could add her name to the deed.

"We'd own it together, you mean," she said.

"Yeah, I guess. Or I could give it to you, outright."

She said she was more concerned with saving for Mark's education. Timothy said he'd look into that, too. They could talk more specifically another time. She could come by the house, or better yet, he could meet her for lunch.

Things began to wind down. Lavinia said she couldn't find the albums. Timothy didn't show Mark the pictures he took from the house a couple of weeks before and was glad now he held off because it was obvious from his relieved expression that he didn't care about that kind of thing.

Lavinia gave Mark a kiss on the cheek, which he wiped off immediately. Then she put her hand under his chin and looked at him lovingly. Timothy couldn't remember her ever looking at him that way. It felt strange, to be jealous of his own son. History was full of similar examples, though. The Roman empire was rife with family discord and avarice, not to mention unsavory behavior. Timothy chuckled.

"What?" Sam asked. She was standing by his lounge chair.

"Nothing. Are you ready to go?"

As he drove them the short distance home, he enjoyed a lovely, mellow mood. He was proud of himself for watching the alcohol so well. He loved how Potter and Lavinia had taken to Mark. He loved the idea of what he could do to help Melissa. And that idea of hers, about taking pictures of people's dining rooms, was just great.

Sam went into the bedroom and changed. She returned in a pair of cut-offs and an oversized T-shirt. Timothy said she looked so nice before. She poured herself a glass of wine and asked him to come outside with her for a while. They could light some citronella candles against the mosquitoes. He grabbed a beer from the fridge and joined her.

She wiped tears from her eyes.

"What's wrong?" he asked, dreading whatever she'd say next. But she said nothing, just cried.

"Is this about you having to drive me home from The Hole last night?" he asked.

Gentle sobbing.

"Something about your poetry?"

No sobbing, just sniffling.

"Was someone mean to you at my mother's?"

She looked at him, her eyes red and glistening.

"I'm sorry," she said.

"For what?"

"Never getting it right."

He looked into the garden, then glanced at her, hoping to see something different, something better. She was the same.

"You took your ring off," he said.

"It's a little too big."

"Get it sized. The guy said it would be free."

"Okay."

"Won't you please tell me what's wrong?"

"I don't know. I just feel like a dog, chasing my tail, running around in circles."

"I get it."

"Do you?"

"Sure."

"Everything seems so easy for you."

"What do you mean by that?"

She said he was used to people covering for him, or at least forgiving him for the hurtful things he did. He started to speak and she held up her hand. She wasn't going to get up in his face about getting drunk at The Hole, though if he recalled, she brought up his drinking a few weeks ago, along with the idea of talking to a therapist to sort out some of his ongoing issues. It was his choice, of course, whether he followed through or not. She hoped he would, or at least explain why he didn't want to, but he said nothing, did nothing. It was hard, dealing with nothing. The way some people found it hard to deal with silence, she supposed. Though to her, silence wasn't as bad as the sense of emptiness that came when you lost touch with someone, or what you thought you understood about them.

"You're talking about me, and our relationship, aren't you?" he asked.

"Obviously."

"But, things are going great."

"Are they?"

"What is this, engagement jitters?"

"That must be it."

"Well, let's not get married until the spring. That will give you plenty of time to plan."

"Plan."

"The wedding, the reception, whatever you have in mind, whatever you want."

She nodded.

A mosquito buzzed by his ear, and he said they forgot to light the candles. She stood up and took care of it. She sat back down. He put his arm around her and said he was sorry things were so stressful, what with meeting Mark and everything. He was certain they'd get used to having him around.

"Do you think he'd like to be my best man?" Timothy asked.

"Oh, I don't know. I assumed you'd ask Foster. Or Matt."

"Not Matt."

The neighbor pulled into his driveway. Loud, rhythmic music filled the air, then stopped.

Timothy asked who she would ask to be her maid of honor.

"Angie, of course," she said.

"And you won't invite your mother?"

"No."

"How about your father?"

"I don't know. I don't want to think about it now."

"Okay."

He said he was going to turn in. She said she wanted to look at that poem she was working on before. If it didn't go anywhere, she'd be right along.

He slept, woke up around two, and saw her side of the bed was empty. The house was dark. Then he heard her in the kitchen, running water in the sink. She still didn't come. He fell back asleep and woke in the morning to find her there, her arms flung over her head and her hair a tangled mass on the pillow.

Chapter Seventeen

On the second Tuesday in August, the temperature topped ninety degrees. Even with the air conditioner on high, the trailer was hot and stuffy. Harcourt brought in a cooler with bagged ice and stuffed water bottles into it. The construction crew got to work early so they could quit early. The sound of their equipment was unusually loud, Timothy thought.

He wished he dragged Sam off to Maine over all her stupid objections. He couldn't imagine a better place to be than on the shore of an ice-cold lake with her at his side.

She was working feverishly on her poetry, trying to assemble the manuscript. Then she was going to that writers' conference over the weekend. Timothy didn't like the idea of her being gone, but then having the house to himself wasn't so bad. For a strange moment, he thought of having Harcourt over for a cook-out, then realized all they'd do was get smashed. What about having Melissa and Mark? And Angie, too? She still hadn't met Mark. He could also call Foster and see if he were free. He'd ask everyone to bring something for the grill, then pick up some salads at the deli. He wasn't about to cook anything, himself.

He didn't mention the barbecue to Sam because she was nervous and distracted. He told her to chill, she'd get her work done on time, and the conference was sure to be fun. She said her professor had arranged for her to give a short reading and she was terrified. She practiced before the mirror and didn't realize how badly she blushed when she was nervous. He said no one would notice and if they did, so what? It was charming, in a way, that rush of color to her face.

She ignored him and kept packing. She wanted to bring clothes for hot days and cool nights. She chose something, put it in the bag, then took it back out. He left her alone.

On Friday morning he saw her off by making her breakfast. She stared at the eggs on her plate, and only had a couple of bites. She tossed and turned all night and looked worn out.

"You're going to do great," he said.

"I hope so."

"Have what's-his-name take pictures."

"Of what?"

"You reading, of course."

"Okay."

Her professor pulled up to the house. Timothy told Sam to ask him in, and she said they were running late. She kissed him and left. He watched her through the window. She opened the rear door of the professor's Jeep and tossed her bag in the back seat. The Jeep let out a plume of smoke as they drove off.

He sent Melissa another text about the barbecue because she hadn't answered the first one a couple of days before. She texted back she'd try to make it, but she wasn't sure what their plans were. Angie said she couldn't come. She and Matt were taking the weekend off from The Hole to go over to Pittsburgh to see his mother. Foster couldn't come, either. He was going camping again.

When he got to the construction trailer, an elderly man was sitting on the couch across from his desk. He introduced himself as Stuart Harcourt, Charles' father. Timothy shook Stuart's hand and said it was a great pleasure to finally meet him. His clothes were tailored and expensive. His loafers alone probably set him back around five hundred bucks, Timothy thought.

"I'm afraid I forgot to tell Charles I was coming today. I seem to have caught him by surprise," Stuart said.

"Where did he run off to?" Timothy asked.

"He had to check on something."

Timothy asked if he could get him some coffee and Stuart said he was just fine, thanks. He was going to wait for Charles to come back and drive him up the hill in the golf cart. The heat and the incline weren't a good idea for someone his age.

"Not that I'm on my last legs, mind you. Just being prudent," Stuart said.

Timothy was met with several emails from prospects he phoned before. Two wanted an appointment; one had bought a house somewhere else, and the other said they decided to wait until spring.

Harcourt returned, looking hot and vexed. He asked his father if he were ready to go. His father stood up without answering and went outside. Harcourt looked at Timothy and rolled his eyes, then left, too.

His phone rang. It was Melissa. She had a huge favor to ask—could Timothy possibly take Mark over the weekend? A friend was in town at the last minute, and she wanted to spend some time with him.

"Sure," Timothy said. He wondered who the friend was and why it was important to see him all of a sudden.

"I appreciate this. I'm sorry about the barbecue. I was waiting to hear from Phil if he'd be in town. He said he couldn't make it, then his plans changed, and now he's coming. I thought it would be fine to have him meet Mark, but then I didn't know. Mark's had a lot of new situations to deal with lately."

So, this guy was another new situation?

"No problem," Timothy said.

"I'll repay the favor, I promise." She said she'd drop Mark off around four, would that work?

"I'll have to leave work early."

"I'm sorry! Phil wants to have an early dinner."

"Sounds like a man with a healthy appetite."

She laughed, then said to give Sam her love. She hung up.

His left temple throbbed. The idea of the whole weekend with his newly met son, without Sam there to act as a buffer, didn't sit well.

There was shouting outside. Timothy opened the door. Harcourt's father stood with a calm, inscrutable expression, while Harcourt waved his arms, then pointed at him and said, "Don't come here and blame me. This was all your idea."

"Gentleman, gentleman, what seems to be the trouble?" Timothy asked in his best take-a-chill-pill voice.

Both men stared at him.

"Your partner doesn't know the first thing about home building, it seems, or about anything else, as far as I can tell," Stuart said.

"Look, we're going to change out those water lines," Harcourt said.

"You were going to take care of that weeks ago," Timothy said.

"I know, I know. Jack said he'd do it."

"How like you, to blame someone else," Stuart said. He said Harcourt would have his answer in the morning.

"Your answer to what?" Timothy asked.

"Ask him. He'll explain it all to you. Just hope what you hear is more or less accurate," Stuart said. He got into his Bentley and drove slowly down the road. Dust rose behind the car.

Harcourt came into the trailer, and Timothy closed the door. His shirt was soaked with sweat. Harcourt sat down and stared into space until Timothy demanded to know what the hell was going on.

"He's going to pull his funding unless I can talk him out of it," Harcourt said.

"What do you mean?"

"It's all his money. I just borrowed it."

"What?"

"He's all ticked off about those stupid plumbing lines, and the other delayed permits. I didn't think he was paying any attention. Turns out he's got someone down at the County who reports on what's going on. Bastard spied on me."

Timothy sat down and asked Harcourt if he had this right: the money Harcourt was using for the project was his father's, and now his father was going to take it back. Where would that leave Timothy and Jack?

"I can still make a go of this. But you guys can't bail on me, not now," Harcourt said.

"You lied."

"No, I didn't. I just didn't go into detail about my funding source."

Timothy put his money in a joint account with Harcourt and Jack. He had the authority to withdraw and deposit funds. He insisted on having that, at Lavinia's urging. Harcourt talked about his father and all his failings while Timothy took out his phone and used the mobile banking app to move his funds out of the joint account and back into his personal one. He told Harcourt what he did.

"What the hell, Dugan, you can't do that!"

"Too late."

"So, you *are* bailing."

"Let's just say I'm giving you an incentive to fix the permitting issues. When you do that and can prove you have, let me know."

It was just like back in college, the way Harcourt slumped and wept softly. Timothy couldn't stand it. He sat at his desk just long enough to forward his company emails to his own account. He worked hard on some of those people and didn't want to let them go. When he reviewed the files and took everything he wanted, he turned the computer off.

Jack came into the trailer. He looked at Timothy.

"What's the deal? The electrician said he's not coming out here today because he never got the check. Did you send it?" he asked.

"You're asking the wrong guy," Timothy said. He went outside, and Jack followed him. Timothy told him what happened.

"Jesus Christ," Jack said.

"Get a lawyer. And keep me posted."

Jack nodded.

When he was in the car, Timothy called Sam and it went to voicemail. He wished she picked up, he needed to talk. Then he called Lavinia. That, too, went to voicemail. When he realized he was heading for The Hole, he turned back and went home. He made himself a sandwich and ate it on the porch. The sky was a searing blue.

He pulled out a new book on King Louis XIV and read for hours. Poor bastard died of gangrene. All that money and entitlement couldn't save him, in the end. The parallel between old Louis and Harcourt galled. Timothy turned his notifications off when he got home, and when he looked at his phone it was full of calls from Harcourt. Timothy hoped he wouldn't show up there, at the house, and beg him to reconsider. Lavinia called back. He punched in her number. When she answered, he laid the whole thing out. She didn't sound surprised. People often got in over their heads. She said he was smart to pull his money, and said it was a good thing he had her lawyer look everything over before he signed. To the best of her recollection, based on a brief conversation she had with him after the fact, Timothy couldn't be sued if Harcourt failed to perform, or displayed gross negligence. And if deliberately using material that failed to pass inspection wasn't gross negligence, she didn't know what was.

"Yup," he said.

"You're on your own this weekend."

"I was, then I agreed to have Mark come and stay."

"Lovely!"

"We'll see."

"I know it's a lot to get used to, but you're doing the right thing by making time for him."

"You don't want to come over and entertain him, do you?"

"Certainly not! Your father and I have plans, anyway."

"Have fun."

"Thanks, you, too."

He tried Sam again, and again it went to voice mail. She was probably all involved with the conference, assuming they arrived. He reckoned the travel time. Yeah, they should be there by now. Maybe she was checking into the hotel or taking a shower.

They had a stash of take-out menus in the kitchen, and he put them on the counter for Mark to look over. Then he realized he hadn't made up the sofa bed in his office. When he went in and pulled it open, it took up almost the whole space. There was no room for him to sit at his computer, but then the bed would only be open when Mark was in it, so it didn't matter.

They should talk about getting a bigger house. Sam wouldn't want to, because she loved their place, but she'd come around. She'd see the logic of it now that Mark was in their lives. A place in the country would suit her, and him, too. A photography studio would take up a small part of it, in an outbuilding, or converted barn. He'd take a hard look at his assets and do some calculations. Lavinia could help him with that. That woman had a keen eye and an innate understanding of money. Sam would write her poems, he'd take photographs. One day, they might turn their place into a sort of artists' colony, a retreat for the brilliant and daring.

And the baby she so desperately wanted? Here, his thinking slowed. That was still an issue, but if she agreed to be the sole caretaker, he thought he could get on board with it.

His phone rang.

"Sorry I didn't answer, before. We just got into town," Sam said.

"You must have taken a detour."

"No, no, we stopped off for lunch."

"Listen, the thing with Harcourt crashed and burned."

"Oh?"

He gave her the summary. In the background, he heard people talking and an occasional laugh. She obviously wasn't calling from her room. He told her about Mark coming for the weekend, and that he made up the sofa bed. Did she have any suggestions about things they could do together until she got back? She said she had to go.

He sat with the phone in his hand for a moment, then put it down.

At exactly four o'clock, Melissa arrived with Mark. One look said Mark didn't want to be there. He didn't meet Timothy's eye as he tromped in with his backpack, which he dropped on the floor in the hall. He went straight into the living room and turned on the television.

Melissa said he was put out about coming over. She was wearing a pale yellow dress and pink sandals. She was like a piece of candy, with hair up in a tight swirl on the back of her head.

"You look fancy," Timothy said.

She laughed nervously, then checked herself in the mirror by the front door. She called out for Mark to be good and listen to his father. A grunt was her reply. Then she left.

Timothy asked Mark to turn off the television set and asked if he brought his Game Boy. Mark said he hadn't, but his laptop was in his pack. He had a cool game on it. They could play it together. Timothy said he wasn't much for video games.

"You hungry?" Timothy asked.

"Yeah."

"We can order something."

"Pizza."

"Not Chinese?"

"I hate Chinese."

"Your mom said you eat everything."

"She doesn't know shit."

"Hey, that's no way to talk."

Mark turned off the television and got his laptop out of his pack.

They ate the pizza outside. Mark asked Timothy why he never come to visit them when they lived in Ohio.

"I didn't know you were there. I didn't even know you were alive," Timothy said and dug out a piece of pepperoni from his back teeth.

Mark said it was okay, it didn't matter. He supposed he could get used to having a dad, and new grandparents, too, of course. He thought Potter was a cool dude. He wasn't so sure about Lavinia.

"She might grow on you," Timothy said.

Timothy asked if Mark minded being an only child and he said sometimes when he thought it would be fun to have a little brother or sister to play with. Maybe his mom would have another kid someday, he didn't know.

"Does she talk about it?" Timothy asked.

"No."

He got himself a beer and another can of Coke for Mark.

"My mom doesn't know this, so don't tell her, but I drink sometimes," Mark said.

"Get out."

"True. She went out one night for dinner, and I had a beer. She didn't even miss it."

"Your mom drinks beer?"

"She keeps it around for Phil in case he comes over."

"Where does Phil live?"

"I don't know. Pennsylvania, maybe."

"What's he like?"

Mark shrugged, but the way he studied his plate said he didn't care for him much. Timothy asked him if he looked forward to school starting next month. Mark said he didn't know. He thought it would be okay.

Timothy's phone rang, and Harcourt's number showed on the screen. Timothy answered. Harcourt launched right into the matter at hand. His father was putting the project on hold. He was going to find another manager and dig up some more venture capital. For the time being Jack, the crew, and of course, Harcourt himself, were out of a job.

"I'm sorry, man. Is there any way your dad will change his mind?" Timothy asked.

"No. He's a hardass. Plus, he hates me. So, I'm up against it, at this point."

Harcourt asked if he could come over. Timothy said he was just on his way out. Harcourt said he got it, they'd get together another time. Then he thanked Timothy for having been willing to take a chance on the project. Timothy said he was sorry it hadn't worked out.

"Who was that?" Mark asked.

"My former business partner."

"What did he want?"

"Aren't you being a little nosy?"

"I'm that way because my mom never tells me anything."

"She told you about me."

"True."

Timothy suggested they watch an old movie. Did Mark know about *Godzilla?* Not the remake, but the original, from the Fifties? Mark asked if Timothy had the Playboy Channel.

"No. And I wouldn't let you watch it if I did."

"I was just kidding."

Neither of them liked the movie much, so Timothy told Mark he could put on whatever he wanted. Mark said he was going to play another game on his laptop and Timothy read his book. The rigid social structure of the court of Versailles sounded nuts, at first, but then it seemed attractive. It would be nice to know where you stood with those around you.

Sam had promised to call him back that evening but didn't. He wanted to hear her voice but wasn't going to bother her. He wondered how Melissa was getting along with Phil, or more importantly, how he was getting along with her. He got himself a short glass of bourbon and read some more but couldn't concentrate. Mark had his headphones in, which spared Timothy the screech of lasers being fired. After a while, Mark said he was tired and wanted to go to bed. Timothy told him where to find a clean towel and asked if he remembered to bring over toothpaste.

"Yeah, I got it," he said.

Alone in the dark, Timothy sat on the porch and listened to the night. The wind rose gently, and now and then a car went down the road. Across the street, a door opened and closed. A cat jumped onto the roof of the shed at the back of the yard and sat a moment before going on its way. After a couple more drinks, he felt relaxed enough to sleep. He cleaned up the kitchen and stuck his head into Mark's room where he was snoring softly.

He woke a few hours later because Sam was sitting on the edge of the bed. It was still dark and for a moment he couldn't remember the day, then as his mind cleared he realized it was early on Saturday and she was supposed to still be at the conference.

"What are you doing here?" he asked. His voice had a strange threadiness to it.

"I came home."

"Why? What happened?"

"I need to talk to you."

She went on sitting. He could see her more clearly now. Her hair was down, and she was in a nice dress with a shawl around her shoulders.

"How did you get here?" he asked.

"I borrowed Steven's car. He'll get a ride back with someone."

"You drove all that way alone?"

"I'm not a child."

He sat up. He forgot to put a glass of water by the bed. He asked if she could bring him one. She didn't turn on any lights as she went through to the kitchen and back. She gave him the glass and sat down on the bed.

"There's no easy way to put this, so I'll speak plainly. I'm leaving you," she said. He held the glass to his lips.

"What?"

"I've been thinking about it all summer."

"I don't believe you."

"It's true."

She said she had a little speech prepared she couldn't for the life of her remember right now, so she was going to have to wing it, but the basic problem was she couldn't go on living with him. He needed to understand it had nothing to do with love, she still loved him and always would, but she needed out. He didn't want her in his life, despite what he might think or tell himself.

"I'll stop drinking," he said. He still hadn't had any of his water, even though his mouth felt like sand.

"You'd have done that by now if you were going to. I don't mean to suggest you never will, only you haven't decided to yet."

He reached to turn on the light and she asked him not to. He asked why she didn't want to see his face. She said it wasn't that. She didn't want him to see hers right now. Sometimes he looked at her so strangely, she thought she might have suddenly become someone else, even something else. He said he didn't understand what she meant, and she said it was impossible to explain.

She saw how he was with Melissa over at his parents' place, and he was still attached to her, or the idea of her. She wasn't sure if he were in love, though she thought so, at first, just as she thought Melissa was in love with him and now didn't think so.

"She's got a boyfriend, after telling me she was going to be on her own, for the foreseeable future," Timothy said, surprised by how much the idea bothered him.

"You should be happy for her, not jealous."

"What does any of this have to do with us?" he asked.

"The fact that there is no 'us.' There hasn't been for a long time. Sometimes I wonder if there ever were."

"You don't believe that! Remember how we were, in the beginning?"

She said of course she did. But then life came along and romance has a hard time surviving against life. Oh, it can, she didn't mean to say otherwise. But you have to fight for love after a while, which means remembering its importance, and the person you associate with it. He didn't associate her with love. He proved that when Melissa came into the picture.

"So, you're leaving me because of her," he said.

"I'm leaving because of you."

Here were the problems: he drank too much and the bigger issue was he didn't seem to understand why. He didn't know what he wanted to do with himself, where he wanted to invest himself, is what she was trying to say.

"I've decided to get deeper into photography," he said.

"That sounds wonderful. I think you'd be good at it."

She sniffed. Was she crying? He didn't think so. Her shoulders slumped when she cried, and they were straight and square, at least as far as he could tell in the dark.

He didn't want children, and that was the biggest problem. Mark was a great surprise, but he wasn't hers, he was Melissa's. She wanted her own child, and she couldn't have one with someone who had no faith that his heart would change. It was okay to be hesitant or uncertain, but most people, or so she believed, felt love for a baby would pull them forward. Love was undeniable. Except for him.

"I know how to love," he said. He put the glass on the bedside table.

"You know how to need. There's a difference."

"Why did you say you wanted to get married?"

"Because I do. But, not to you."

"You went along with it. You made people think we were going to."

"I know. And I shouldn't have. The point you're missing, or I'm afraid you're missing, is you don't want to marry me."

"Sam, I do want to marry you."

"You only proposed because you needed something to hang on to and give your life direction. I can't do that for you. You have to do that for yourself."

He tried to think but the blood thudding in his ears was too loud. He had to use the toilet, so he got up and went. He listened for Mark and heard nothing. Sam hadn't moved. He sat next to her on the bed. Up close, she smelled of sweat and perfume. His heart surged, and he held her. She allowed it for a moment, then withdrew from his embrace.

She had to think about the future, she said. There was the baby, that was one thing, but there was also her poetry. She thought she could make it as a poet, and she wanted to be with someone who supported her.

"You don't think I do?" he asked.

"You put up with it, you don't object to it, but no, you don't support it."

He didn't understand how lonely she was all summer, thinking all of this. In case he was worried, she hadn't said anything to anyone in the family. She would when the time came. Finally, she shared her thoughts with Steven, and she was glad she did because that allowed him to share things with her, too, things she was glad to know.

"Yeah, like what?" Timothy asked.

"He loves me."

"Are you kidding me?"

"Why is that impossible?"

"The guy's what, fifty?"

"Forty-two."

"Have you been …?"

"Having an affair? No, but we were about to, on this trip, and that's when I realized I needed to come home and tell you the truth about how I feel."

"Are you in love with him?"

"I think I am. But that's not why I'm leaving you. I'm leaving you for all the reasons I just said."

His tears shocked him. He leaned forward with his face in his hands. Her arms went around him, and he leaned into her, crying so hard his breathing was ragged and rough. She didn't let go even when he eased. She didn't speak or try to comfort him, just let him be there in his grief and distress.

He wanted to ask her not to go, to give them another chance. He wanted to say so many things and couldn't. He lay on the bed and she lay next to him, her hand in hers. Neither spoke nor slept, just stayed like that together, breathing, waiting, until the light dared show itself between the blind and window frame. She sat up, said something about being in touch soon to work out some details, and stood over him in the faint light. He could see her now, and she'd never been so solid and beautiful.

Then she was gone.

THE END

About the Author

Anne Leigh Parrish lives in a forest in the South Sound Region of Washington State. She is the author of twelve previously books which include short stories, novels, and poems. She has recently ventured into the art of photography. Find her online at anneleighparrish.com.

About Unsolicited Press

Unsolicited Press is based out of Portland, Oregon, and focuses on the works of the unsung and underrepresented. As a womxn-owned, all-volunteer small publisher that doesn't worry about profits as much as championing exceptional literature, we have the privilege of partnering with authors skirting the fringes of the lit world. We've worked with emerging and award-winning authors such as Shann Ray, Amy Shimshon-Santo, Brook Bhagat, Kris Amos, and John W. Bateman.

Learn more at unsolicitedpress.com. Find us on Twitter and Instagram @UnsolicitedP.